IRRESISTIBLE

Richard Scrimger

Illustrations by Britt Wilson

Scholastic Canada Ltd.
Toronto New York London Auckland Sydney
Mexico City New Delhi Hong Kong Buenos Aires

To you, with the book in your hand. Yes you.
You're welcome.
— R.S.

Scholastic Canada Ltd.
604 King Street West, Toronto, Ontario M5V 1E1, Canada

Scholastic Inc.
557 Broadway, New York, NY 10012, USA

Scholastic Australia Pty Limited
PO Box 579, Gosford, NSW 2250, Australia

Scholastic New Zealand Limited
Private Bag 94407, Botany, Manukau 2163, New Zealand

Scholastic Children's Books
Euston House, 24 Eversholt Street, London NW1 1DB, UK

www.scholastic.ca

Library and Archives Canada Cataloguing in Publication

Title: Irresistible / Richard Scrimger ; illustrations by Britt Wilson.

Names: Scrimger, Richard, 1957- author. | Wilson, Britt, 1986- illustrator.

Description: Series statement: The Almost Epic Squad

Identifiers: Canadiana (print) 20190060964 | Canadiana (ebook) 20190061030 |
ISBN 9781443157889 (hardcover) | ISBN 9781443157896 (ebook)

Classification: LCC PS8587.C745 I77 2019 | DDC jC813/.54—dc23

Illustrations and hand lettering by Britt Wilson.
Cover background image copyright © Piotrurakau/Getty Images.

6 5 4 3 2 1   Printed in Canada 114   19 20 21 22 23

MIX
Paper from
responsible sources
FSC® C016245

THE EMERGENCY LIGHTING SYSTEM OVERLOADS!

Z-Z+

KSSHH

FSS+

A CLOUD OF GLOWING DUST RAINS DOWN ONTO THE SLEEPING BABIES.

BEEP BEEP BEE

BABY FLEM GETS A NOSEFUL.

BABY LUNDBORG IS SPRINKLED DOWN THE SPINE.

THE RIGHT SIDE OF BABY KILDARE'S CRANIUM IS DUSTED.

BABY O'KAYE SWALLOWS A MOUTHFUL.

2

REIDIUM (ATOMIC NUMBER 13½):
AN INCREDIBLY RARE AND VOLATILE
ELEMENT. WHEN REFINED WITH
GARLIC, IT HAS HUGE ENERGY
POTENTIAL. BUT AFTER SEVERAL
DISASTERS, INDUSTRIES DEEMED
IT TOO DANGEROUS. SOME
REIDIUM REMAINS, IN THE
REMOTE MOUNTAINS OF PIANVIA
AND HERE IN SLEEPY DIMLY.

THESE BABIES COULD CHANGE THE WORLD!

THE HOSPITAL STILL USES DIMLY REIDIUM BULBS! I'VE DONE REIDIUM EXPERIMENTS ON RODENTS.

AND . . .

MEET MY LAB ASSISTANTS.

THIS IS STAN. AND THERE'S DAPHNE, CLAUDE, ELAINE, AL . . . AND GERALD.

UH. HELLO?

TIME FOR THE BABIES TO GO HOME.

WHAT A VOICE HE HAS!

AAAAAAAHH

WWA

WHAT?

THEIR SPECIAL POWERS MAY NOT SHOW UNTIL PUBERTY. THAT'S HOW IT WAS WITH THE MICE. BUT THEN THEY'LL BE EPIC!

TILL THEN THEY'RE ... WELL ... ALMOST EPIC!

FASSBINDER AND NUSSBAUM PRESS ON AS A TEAM. MORE THAN ONE KIND OF SPARK FLIES.

BUT LOVE DOESN'T KEEP YOU IN GARLIC. DESPERATE FOR FUNDING, FASSBINDER CONTACTS SECRET GOVERNMENT DEPARTMENT C, IN CHARGE OF PROBLEMS NO ONE ELSE TAKES SERIOUSLY.

FUTURE SUPERPOWERS ARE LIKELY!

FROM: DEPARTMENT C
TO: DR. FASSBINDER
SUBJECT: FUNDING (NOT MUCH) APPROVED.

FINALLY, AFTER ALL THESE YEARS. A CHANCE TO PROVE ...

I MUST GO. THE WORK IS IMPORTANT.

THERE'S ONLY FUNDING FOR ONE.

BUT WHAT ABOUT US?

NOTHING REMAINS BUT THE STENCH OF SCORCHED RUBBER-SOLED NURSING SHOES.

OR SO IT SEEMS . . .

DR. FASSBINDER AND HIS ASSISTANTS CONTINUE THEIR EXPERIMENTS IN A TOP-SECRET LAB IN MONTREAL, TESTING THE CHILDREN FOR "GIFTED" EVERY YEAR . . .

MEANWHILE, SOMEONE KNOWN ONLY AS "THE BOSS" QUIETLY RECRUITS A TEAM OF NEFARIOUS MINIONS TO SHADOW THE ALMOST EPIC KIDS . . .

. . . AND TAKES TO THE SKIES IN A TATTERED BLIMP. EVER ANGRY, EVER EVIL, EVER SMELLING OF BURNT RUBBER, AND IMPATIENTLY AWAITING THE CHILDREN AND THEIR POWERS.

BUT WHAT OF THE CHILDREN TODAY?

CHAPTER 1

WHY ARE WE STARTING HERE?

"Call that a dress? It looks like pudding."

"Pudding, Arch? That's your best insult?"

"Chocolate pudding. The buttons are like whipped cream."

"Don't think mean thoughts. What you think, you become. Anyway, I'm dressed up to go to a symposium after your fun party."

"Call this fun? Geez, Dale. Uday over there is so bored he looks like he's been run over by a funeral. Party? I've seen happier teeth."

"Teeth?"

"I mean the things you get in your teeth."

"Cavities? Braces? Root canals?"

"Yeah."

"But you've never had a root canal, Arch. You're thirteen. You still have baby teeth."

"I'm mature for my age. I— Oh no! Oh no! Help!"

Oops. My bad. I was at the door talking to my landlady, and the story started without me. (I'm behind in my rent, and Mrs. Ravioli was mad. I couldn't slam the door in her face.) You don't know what's going on, or who's talking, do you? Oh dear. This is embarrassing. Let's set the scene. Ready? *Ahem.*

It's a Thursday afternoon in May, and it's gorgeous! Vancouver is one of the prettiest cities in the world when it's sunny, and it's sunny today. Archie O'Kaye is having his thirteenth birthday party on the rooftop terrace of his dad's downtown condo. We're talking crystal and granite inside the party room, and a giant sparkly patio outside, with views of mountains and ocean and white towers and Chinatown and all that

Vancouver stuff. So, there's our setting: pretty city, sunny May afternoon, thirteenth birthday party.

What else does a story need? Characters. Archie's folks are divorced. His dad is named Ryan. He sells real estate, drives a sports car and says *man* a lot. He's pretty dull. You'll meet Mom tomorrow. Maeve. She's way more fun, with a wide happy mouth and hair like freedom. (Does that sound weird? I hope not. I like Archie's mom. I know I'm just the narrator, but I do.)

Shanaya the waitress is not important to the story, but she will show up again. She shops in the same organic market as one of the baddies.

Archie and Dale and Uday are our main guys. What's with them? This is Archie's story. He's the hero so I'll start with him. He's a mess. He has uncombed hair, an unwashed face, an untucked shirt and droopy socks. He's a bit of a baby. A bit? A lot. He cares mostly about himself — the way babies do — and he says what he thinks — also the way babies do. He was one of those four kids in the maternity ward of Dimly General Hospital thirteen years ago.

Archie has an appointment with Dr. Fassbinder in Montreal in two days. (You remember him from the comic at the front of this book, right? Moustache and glasses and lab coat — interested in reidium — that guy.) Dr. Fassbinder thinks Archie might be special. Most people think he's a dork, and most of the time, well, they're right. Dale and Uday are the only kids at this birthday party because Archie has managed to bore or tick off everyone else. Dr. Fassbinder is right too — Archie is special. We'll get to that later.

Dale talks slowly in a deep voice. She likes to quote the Buddha, and cares about things like climate change and homeless people and endangered species. Good things, you know? Causes. That symposium she's going to later is about chakras. The speaker is a guru who's been on TV with Oprah. Dale will be handing out lotus flowers afterwards. To look at, Dale is thin like a twig, with long fingers and toes and chin. She can walk on her hands. She bends in every direction, like one of those inflatable tube guys in front of car dealerships. Only she moves slower. *Does she do yoga?* you ask. Come on. Does it get dark at night?

As far as Uday is concerned, it's never dark around Dale — for him, the sun rises and sets on her. Not that feelings get in the way of Uday's ambition. He's a hustler, a mover, a smiling, big-eyed dreamer. Or maybe *schemer* is a better word. He lives with his mom, dad, little sister and homesick nani. Uday rolls his eyes when Nani starts talking about the old country. He was born in Vancouver. He doesn't speak

Urdu. He can't find Hyderabad on a map. He can barely spell it.

Uday doesn't like Archie much. But Dale is Archie's friend, and Uday likes Dale — I mean, he *really* likes her. He'll do anything to be near her, even go to that chakra symposium (which he will think is sooooooo booooooooooring). Even go to Archie's party.

So, why is Dale a friend of Archie's? Good question. Archie doesn't care about the planet or the poor or the chakras. He's self-absorbed and not always very nice. Heck, I don't like him that much and I'm the narrator.

But Dale really likes Archie. Why? He can be funny sometimes. And he says what he thinks, even if it's not polite. If he thinks your shoes look silly, he'll say so, which isn't nice. But it means you can trust him. He's never going to lie to you. Which is a bigger kind of nice. Is that enough? I don't know. *Liking* is an odd business. You don't *decide* to like someone any more than you *decide* to like baseball or zombie movies or black licorice. It just happens.

Okay, enough about setting and characters. It's time for action. Why does the story start here? Why not last week or last month? Why not a couple of days from now, when Archie flies to Montreal for his yearly checkup?

Because this party marks the first time Archie's superpower is going to show itself. You saw the comic at the beginning of the story, right? Like Jessica and Gary and Daisy, the other kids in the Dimly maternity ward, Archie's been watched since birth to see if his power kicks in at puberty. It's right now, in fact. I said we'd get back to the plot. Here we go.

"Oh no! Oh no! Help!" says Archie.

He's screaming because a bird has flown up to the terrace and is flapping right at him.

Don't go thinking eagles and pterodactyls. It's not that kind of bird. It's little and brownish. It's interested in Archie because it's building a nest, and Archie's messy hair looks like a lot of straw. So the bird pecks at him. Dale tries to gently shoo it away, but it won't leave Archie alone. And Archie gets scared.

He runs inside, covering his head, and turns into a superhero.

CHAPTER 2

ARCHIE O'KAYE = WOW!

Not a real superhero. But almost. Here's how it goes down. Archie's panicking. *Why is this bird picking on me?* he thinks. *Why won't it leave me alone? Oh no, oh no, oh no!* (Sorry. I know he's our hero. But he's not very brave.)

Archie gets scared a lot. This time is different. This time, when he gets scared he feels something happen inside him. Something apart from fear is filling him up. He doesn't know what it is. But I do. And I'll tell you. It's *charm*. Weird, eh? Sweet liquid charm pours out of Archie's glands, filling the nooks and crannies of his body, displacing the horrible emptiness of fear. Archie fills with charm the way a car fills with gas.

When Dr. Bruce Banner gets mad, he turns into

the Hulk. He's unstoppable. It's sort of like that with Archie. When he gets scared now, on his thirteenth birthday, he turns incredibly charming. When the level of charm rises to his throat, he talks the way he feels, which is . . . *irresistible.*

The waitress is the first to notice.

Did I tell you her name? It's Shanaya. She's the first one to sense the change in Archie. When he runs inside she thinks, *That dorky birthday boy is more interesting than I thought.* He seems taller now, like he's standing straighter and on tiptoe and sucking in his stomach. His hair is neater. His eyes are bigger, rounder, wetter and deeper. He's a different person.

He opens his mouth, and—

And—

And—

And—

"Well … uh … *hello*, there."

"*Grrp.*" That's all Shanaya can say. The voice hypnotizes her. She moves toward it, holding the pizza tray in front of her like an offering.

"Excuse me," says the other boy at the party, the skinny guy who looks like her cousin Abhay. "Pardon me. You may not be aware of it, but as a matter of fact I was reaching for—"

Shanaya ignores him. "Please," she offers the tray. "Please, please, o wonderful birthday boy, please take something. Anything."

Dale doesn't see any of this. She's busy waving her arms, getting the bird out of the way. When she comes inside, Archie has his back to her. She can't see his face. She doesn't understand why the waitress and Uday and Mr. O'Kaye are all staring as if he has sprouted a halo.

"I have to leave now," Dale says. "My symposium starts in fifteen minutes."

At her words, Archie's world comes back to normal. He's not afraid of Dale. His fear leaves him. And so does the charm. Just like the Hulk's muscles when he's not angry anymore. His hair rumples again. His shirt comes undone.

"What – what – just happened – to me?" he says, his voice starting as a squeak and ending as a growl.

Uday blinks. Mr. O'Kaye fingers his earring and mutters, "Man, oh man."

The waitress shakes her head. Why is her mouth dry? Why is her heart beating so wildly? "Want a slice of pizza?" she asks.

He frowns at the tray. "Call that pizza?"

The party ends shortly. Dale and Uday head off to the chakra symposium. Archie goes downstairs to pack for his trip to Montreal. The waitress carries the trays and cloths and leftovers into the caterer's van. *What a weird party,* she thinks. That kid — Archie, they called him. The cheque is signed Ryan O'Kaye, so the boy is Archie O'Kaye.

She drives down Main Street, thinking, *Archie O'Kaye = wow.*

CHAPTER 3

BORED MUCH?

Let's skip a couple of days and across the country. A late flight from Vancouver to Montreal with a stopover in Winnipeg, Archie yawning the whole way, even when his mom points out the hot-air balloon floating low to the ground near the Winnipeg airport.

"Remember that blimp from when we lived in Manitoba, Arch?" Maeve asks.

SCARY MUSIC

"No."

"I wonder if it's the same blimp? And who it belongs to?"

SCARY MUSIC

"Not me. I don't wonder about the blimp or anything else."

SCARY MUSIC

Did you hear that? There's something sinister about that blimp.

SCARY MUSIC

I thought so. Every time I mention it we get the scary music. I'm not putting it in on purpose. It's part of the story.

Now 9:00 a.m. Montreal time, in a Montreal taxi. Archie is still getting used to the time change, so it feels like six in the morning. The taxi smells of his mom's perfume, which is comforting, but it also smells of old sweat and older cab driver, which is yuck.

Montreal is not like any other city in North America. "A piece of Europe on the other side of the Atlantic" is how someone (I don't know who) described it. Archie's mom draws his attention to the French road signs, to the *tabacs* and *dépanneurs* on the street corners, to the curved staircases leading to the front doors of the houses.

"There's so much that's different here," she says. "Isn't it wonderful, Arch?"

"What's so good about different?" he replies sulkily. "I want what I like. A doughnut. Eh? Where's the doughnut shops?"

His mom sighs. She feels guilty. Dr. Fassbinder flies her son across the country every year to check for giftedness. It has to be a mistake. Her darling boy is not like the other gifted kids she knows. His marks in school are worse than theirs. He can't run fast, or add, or carry a tune. He can't dance a tango or dunk a basketball. He gets lots of cavities. He doesn't pay a lot of attention to anything except food and video games and, well, himself. He's scared of animals — especially insects and birds.

He says what he thinks, even if it's impolite. One time his nana pointed out a stain on Archie's cheek and he didn't thank her, or apologize, or try to wipe it off. He just shrugged. "I don't have to look at it — you do," he said. Funny, yes, but rude.

Is bad behaviour a gift? Maeve Whelan doesn't want to waste the doctor's time or money. She wonders if the Dimly General Hospital made a mistake when her boy was born. Should Dr. Fassbinder be studying someone else?

"Almost there, Arch," she says.

"Uh-huh." He stares down at his lap. He seems fascinated by his fingers.

The cab stops at the downtown hospital. It's his second day of testing. Maeve tips the driver handsomely and climbs out, smoothing her skirt, smiling bravely. "Come on, Arch. The doctor's waiting."

Into the hospital, down to the sub-basement, along

a dusty corridor to a dingy door marked *Institut de l'ennui / Boredom Institute.* (The name is short for: Building On Reidium — Extra Degrees of Mightiness!)

The waiting room is empty. Archie throws himself onto a chair while his mom signs in for him.

"Do you want me to stay, Arch?" she asks. "Or are you okay on your own? There's a coffee shop upstairs. I could meet you there when you're done."

"Yeah, go to the coffee shop and buy me a dough-nut. Great idea!"

"I think I can do that, Arch."

"I like Boston cream best. And you should get one for yourself too."

"Why, Arch, you're thinking of me! How nice of you!"

He blinks. "I'm thinking you never finish your doughnut, so I'll get most of it. That's sort of like thinking of you."

She laughs. "Sort of."

☆ ☆ ☆

Four thousand kilometres away, in an organic market in south Vancouver, Shanaya is on the phone with her sister. They're talking about the birthday party from a couple of days ago.

"I can't stop thinking about it, and about . . . *him*!" Shanaya says, throwing a half-dozen Hungry Vegan dinners into the cart. "The birthday boy. Most of the party he was a pest. And then he transformed into the coolest guy in the world. A superhero. Or what's-his-name with the hair from that band. You know who I mean. That guy. It was like magic."

One aisle away from Shanaya, well within earshot, stands a frightening figure. No, "stands" is the wrong word. The tall woman does not stand — she hunches over her cane. Seriously, she is bent so far over that she looks like a question mark.

?

Like that.

She's buying chokeberry, tickseed, dumb cane, mugwort, spatterdock, navelwort, wingnut, pokeweed, bloodroot, bladderwort, wormwood and toadflax to put in her salad.

Yes, those are all real plants.

Clementine "the Crutch" Clutterbucket was not always like this. Thirteen years ago she was the upright and ambitious Nurse Clutterbucket, assigned to the maternity ward of the Dimly General Hospital. Back then she stood tall and straight, smiled often and ate happy salads full of maidenhair, morning glory, windflower, yellow rocket, gold blossom, bachelor's buttons, summersweet, wintersweet and starflower.

Yes, these are real plants too. I'm not going to lie to you. I'm the narrator. You can believe me.

So, what happened to Clementine? you ask. Good question. She and Nurse Debbie Nussbaum, her boss, were both interested in the special light bulbs in the Dimly maternity ward. These bulbs used a dangerous element called reidium, and their boss, Dr. Fassbinder, was studying the effects of reidium. After he left for Montreal, Nurse Nussbaum devised her own experiment involving superheated reidium, which promptly exploded, vaporizing the lab totally and destroying most of the office next door as well. The desk and chair disappeared, along with part of Nurse Clutterbucket's spine. (She was sitting in the chair.)

The operation to fuse the rest of her together resulted in a hunched appearance and sour disposition. For thirteen years, ever since the explosion, Clementine Clutterbucket has walked with a cane, and hated Dr. Fassbinder and the four children he was studying. She works for her old boss, who flies around the country in a tattered blimp.

SCARY MUSIC

Hey, did you hear that? Same music we heard when Maeve noticed the blimp—

SCARY MUSIC

—at the Winnipeg airport. Huh. Happens every time I mention it. Anyway, for thirteen years, Clementine "the Crutch" Clutterbucket has made her salads from bitter weeds.

Now, back to the story.

"The kid put us under a spell," Shanaya says into the phone. "It was like he had a superpower. Mr. Charm. I would have done anything he asked."

Clementine "the Crutch" hobbles up to a stock clerk and asks if they have any fresh sneezeweed. (Yes, it's real too.) The clerk goes in the back to check. Shanaya moves to the checkout now. She laughs into her phone as she unloads her cart.

"I'll never forget the kid's name," she tells her sister. "The one with that sudden superpower. Archie O'Kaye. Isn't that wonderful? A-OK, you know? He's A-OK with me, I have to tell you."

In the next aisle, Clementine hears Shanaya say Archie's name clearly. She gasps. Archie O'Kaye was one of the four children back in Dimly. The Boss assigned Clementine to track him. She followed the O'Kayes to Vancouver, and then lost them in the big city. That was five years ago. Could there be two Archie O'Kayes?

When the stock clerk comes back with the fresh sneezeweed, Clementine is gone.

CHAPTER 4

CALL THAT A GIFT?

Back in Montreal, in the basement Boredom Institute, Archie has almost finished this year's tests for his giftedness. He's written a logic quiz, and had his muscles probed and reflexes checked. He's jumped, lifted weights, run on a treadmill, held his breath. Now he's putting his shirt back on.

"Hoawmmmm," says Dr. Fassbinder, checking the screens. "Below average in everything again. But don't feel bad, Archie."

"Eh? Why should I?" says Archie. "*Me* feel bad? You're the one running these stupid tests. You're the one who should feel bad. Ha ha ha. Call those tests? Ha ha ha. The only test they pass is the smell test — eh? Speaking of smelly, if that kid with the runny nose is gifted, I'm an aardvark. And Daisy from my school. She comes here too, right? What's with her? Everyone's a loser. At least I'm normal."

"Actually, Archie, you are below normal." The doctor pulls at his moustache. He's got a beauty, curled up around his nose.

"So, I guess I must be *extra* qualified for your study then, eh?" Archie starts to laugh some more but gets distracted by his hands. He turns them into giant crab claws. *Snap snap snap.* "Hah! Take that!" He attacks the doctor's arm with his crab claws.

The doctor sighs and spins in his chair to finish the interview. "Two more questions, Archie. Have you noticed anyone paying attention to you? Following you around? Maybe someone from back in Dimly?"

"Eh?" says Archie. He says this a lot.

"How about a hot-air balloon. Have you ever looked up and seen one of those, closer than it should be?"

"A blimp?"

SCARY MUSIC (Yup. There it is.)

"Like at a baseball game? Following me? I dunno. I doubt it. Who'd pay attention to me? And anyway, why would I notice? I don't spend my time looking up."

"Why indeed." The doctor sighs again. "All right. Last question. You are thirteen years old now. Lots of hormones. Puberty is a time of great change: bones, hair, muscles, voice. Have you noticed any gifts that today's tests might not be able to pick up? Has anything strange happened to you?"

"You mean, can I fly or turn invisible? Eh? That kind of gift?"

"Yes, yes. Just like that."

"Or shoot lasers out of my eyes? Or tell what someone else is thinking? Ho ho ho. Let's check now. What are *you* thinking, Doc? Wait. Wait! Don't move. I'm getting a signal . . ." Archie puts his finger to his forehead and closes his eyes, pretending to concentrate. "Wow. Maybe I do have a gift, because I know what you're thinking right now. You're thinking: *Geez that Archie O'Kaye is a real dork. I never want to see him again!*"

Dr. Fassbinder almost smiles. "Are you sure you don't have telepathic powers? Because that guess was very close." He has an accent that stretches all his vowel sounds, so that "very" comes out sounding like "vaairy." And "close" is more like "clooase." You'll have to imagine all those extra letters while he's talking. I'm not going to write them out. It would take too long. I'd be an old man by the time I finished writing the book, my white whiskers falling over the keyboard.

"Doc," says Archie, "if I could turn myself invisible, I wouldn't be here, would I? I'd be robbing a candy store. Or pranking Big Mean Ehsin. Yeah! I'd sneak up behind him and tie his shoelaces together. He'd fall down and look around for the bad guy, and I'd be invisible. Ho ho ho. That's what I'd be doing if I had a superpower."

"Yeasss, you probably would," says the doctor, making a quick note on a file. The note reads: "A. O'Kaye. No talent. Self-absorbed. Unformed personality — like a baby. Most unlikeable child I ever met. Do not schedule for next year. Never wish to see him again."

"Weeall, I guess we're done here," says Dr. Fassbinder. "My assistants will tidy up when you leave. I don't know what we will decide to do next year. Perhaaaaps—" He breaks off when Archie screams. "What's wrong?"

"Eek!" Archie stands on his chair, pointing down at the floor. One, two, four furry little creatures have dashed out from under the doctor's desk. "Mice!" Archie shrieks. "I can't stand mice! I – I –"

The doctor chuckles. "Don't be afraid, Archie. These are my assistants. They have helped me for some years now. Good afternoon, Marvin, Denise, Elaine. And Claude, of course. You are all up early today."

The mice wear lab coats. Two carry clipboards. The one named Claude waves a teeny paw.

"What?" says Archie. "What– what –"

The doctor explains: "These mice were exposed to reidium when they were young. Look what it's done to them. They are almost a different species — supermice. Claude is quite the linguist — speaks three human languages as well as Mussine. And they've all exceeded their expected lifespan. Why, some of them are older than you, Archie. These little fellows have taught me so much about the properties of reidium. And I've been interested in you and Gary and Daisy and Jessica ever since *your* reidium exposure. I have high hopes for the girls. I don't know about Gary yet. I see him again in a few minutes. But in your case, Archie, I just don't seem to be able to locate any kind of super—"

Dr. Fassbinder breaks off abruptly and stares at Archie as he climbs down from his chair. The boy's hair is neater. Somehow, his shirt is tucked in. His smile is as white and magnetic as the North Pole.

"Hi... I mean, hello... there... How are you? *All* of you?" Archie says to the mice. Adrenalin courses through his body. And it has happened again. As it did at his birthday party, fear has activated Archie's special power.

"How... totally *wonderful* to meet you all," he says, bending low.

There is a collective high-pitched gasp. A mouse with a clipboard squeaks, then ducks her head bashfully.

"Eek, yourself," says Archie, smiling broadly. "You are totally wonderful, do you know that? What's *your* name?"

"E–laine," she squeaks.

"That's a lovely name. Like music. It suits you. And *you*, Claude, with the twitchy ears. What a rogue you are. Keep your eye on *this* one, Doctor." Archie bends further and pokes the mouse with a gentle forefinger.

Claude squeaks contentedly. Archie straightens up.

Dr. Fassbinder has been typing rapidly all this time. Now he rises to his feet. "You . . ." he begins.

"No, no, it's *you*, Doctor." Archie faces him. "I simply can't thank you *enough* for . . . all you've done. I'm just terribly sorry to have . . . well . . . let you down."

"No, no, no," says the doctor, breathing deeply. "Not at all, Archie. I am delighted to see you. Truly. This has been a wonderful visit. I've enjoyed every second."

"You're . . . really . . . too kind. All of you are. I can't *wait* to, uh, come back. I'm sure we'll have great times together, all of us. While we work out what it is — if anything — that I can do well." He favours them with a particularly melodious chuckle.

The doctor finds himself laughing along. "No worries there. We're happy to spend time in your company, Archie. Right, boys and girls?"

"Oh yes," the mice all squeak together.

"Come back next year," squeaks Elaine.

Archie wags his finger at her. "You just *try* to keep me away." He gives an infectious laugh. They all catch the infection and join in.

Archie leaves the room. Dr. Fassbinder shakes his head to clear it. It takes him a few seconds to recall what has just happened. Right! The boy Archie O'Kaye has finished his testing for this year. And what exactly did the tests prove? The doctor checks his onscreen file notes, which now read: "A. O'Kaye. Amazing potential. Could do anything. Most likeable child I ever met. Must see again next year. Reminder to Dept. C to book him first-class tickets. Check his hotel status."

As Archie walks down the hall, the adrenalin drains out of him like dirty bathwater. He breathes out, shakes his hands, lets his shoulders relax. The back of his shirt begins to blouse out of his pants. When he reaches the door at the end of the hall, he is moving toward normal.

The boy in the waiting room is long and lean. He tosses a Kleenex at the wastebasket.

Archie compliments the boy's shooting. "That juke to the right? *Sweet.* You could be a three-point king," he says. There's still some charm remaining in his voice, like heat in a dying ember.

Archie shakes his head and his hair comes uncombed. His shirttail is flapping by now. He is back to his usual inappropriate self. He continues. "If you had any talent. Call that a shot? I've seen better at the flu clinic."

The kid's face falls like rain.

Archie heads out the door.

CHAPTER 5

THE SEER

Maeve has not forgotten the Boston creams. She sits with her cup of cooling coffee, playing poker on her phone. Yeah, she's pretty cool. When Archie arrives, he checks under the table, then pulls a chair over.

"Whoa — chocolate milk too? Way to go, Mom." He rubs his hands together and starts in.

"How was the test?" Maeve asks. "Did you learn anything?"

"The lab has mice." He shivers. "I hate mice."

"For experiments?"

"They had lab coats."

"What? The mice?"

"One of them speaks three languages." His mouth is full of doughnut.

Maeve sighs and shakes her head. Her boy has an active imagination but no gift.

A bald eight-year-old in a bathrobe walks into the hospital coffee shop. She's between her parents, who look tired and sad. The girl comes right up to Maeve and gives her a gap-toothed smile.

"You're nice," she says. Which is true. Maeve is nice. "Will you be my friend?" she lisps. "Mommy says I need friends right now."

Maeve and the girl's mom share a glance.

"Sure, honey." Maeve dabs at her eyes. "I'll be your friend. My name is Maeve. What's yours?"

"Sibyl," says the girl. "It means I am a seer." She turns to Archie. Her smile fades.

"I see that you're special," she says. "That's what I see."

He looks up from his doughnut. "I see you're bald."

All the adults gasp. "Arch!" says Maeve. "That's not nice."

"It isn't? Why? She is bald. Look at her."

He doesn't know why Sibyl is bald. Maybe you do. But you spend more time thinking about other people than Archie does. He says what he thinks, but he doesn't think about very much. Except himself.

"My body is a battlefield," says Sibyl. "That's what my doctor says. Is your body a battlefield?"

"No. But my hands are claws. Ha! Ha!" Archie makes snapping motions at the arm of Sibyl's bathrobe. She laughs. Her parents lead her away, still laughing.

"That's why you're special," she says, over her shoulder.

I'd like to stay with Archie and his mom. Like Sibyl, Maeve could use a friend right now. But I have a story to tell, and it's time to get back to the bad guys.

CHAPTER 6

THE BIG BOSS

Remember the scary music? We've had it a couple of times. Whenever I type the word "blump."

No. Not this time. What? Why not? What did I—

Oh. I just saw. I mistyped. I meant to type "blimp."

SCARY MUSIC

Yup. There it is. It belongs to Clementine Clutterbucket's boss.

We left Clementine "the Crutch" buying sneezeweed. Now we're back. When she overhears Archie O'Kaye's name, she drops her shopping basket and crutches herself past the checkout. In the parking lot she sees a young woman getting into a van with *Vancouver's Best Catering* on the door. Clementine hobbles over to the van and raps on the driver's window.

"Where was that party?" she asks in her piercing voice.

"I beg your pardon?" says Shanaya the waitress.

"Where was the party with Archie O'Kaye?"

Shanaya stares out at the witchy old lady bent over so far she looks like a question mark. "Do *you* know him?"

"I was his very first babysitter. Thirteen years ago."

"Really? Wow. What was he like back then?"

"But I lost track of him. Tell me, where does he live now?"

Five minutes later, Clementine is in a cab on her way home. She lives at the end of 66th Street — number 6, in fact — in south Vancouver. It's a small house with a big basement and what looks like the tallest flagpole in town in the backyard. It isn't a flagpole, though. It's a mooring mast.

Clementine heaves herself inside and downstairs to her computer to talk to her boss, the former Nurse Debbie Nussbaum from the Dimly General Hospital maternity ward. When her reidium experiment backfired, Nurse Nussbaum disappeared from the hospital staff — and from everywhere else as well. The blast made her invisible. She has used that superpower well, building a business empire based on secrets she overheard when no one knew she was there, on proposals she read over their authors' shoulders, on decisions made at board meetings she was not invited to. One of her first hires was her fellow experimenter.

Clementine sets up a video session. As usual, there is a moment of surprise when the call goes through and Clementine sees her boss.

"Is this about *Goodlitewow!*?"

Clementine turns up the volume.

"No, Boss. *Goodlitewow!* is still underperforming. I'm trying to work out why. This is something else."

"What is more important than *Goodlitewow!*?"

"I've found Archie O'Kaye."

"Ahhhhhhh."

Nurse Nussbaum's vocal cords may have been injured in the reidium explosion. Hard to say, because no doctor has ever examined her. But for the last thirteen years — ever since the blast — she has spoken in a raspy, whispery voice. It always sounds like she's hissing. (You might think "Ahhhhhhh" is hard to hiss, but The Boss has no trouble.)

Clementine never knows what to expect to see on the Skype camera. The Boss is invisible but her clothes aren't, and she dresses differently for every session. Tonight she wears a Guy Fawkes mask — white face, skinny moustache and chin beard, big smile. Her shoulders are draped in a black coat.

"Aha," she hisses. "Tell me more."

"I spoke to the waitress at a birthday party for someone named Archie O'Kaye. This is the fourth potential Archie I've found, but this one's birthdate matches up to the very week. It was his thirteenth birthday, so if he's the right Archie, his superpower should be developing soon. I don't know if he has one yet. The waitress said he was really nice."

"Nice is not a superpower." The Skype image shudders. Nussbaum's shoulders shake with rage. Or maybe it's turbulence.

"Where are you tonight?" asks Clementine.

The Boss has barely set foot on the ground in years. She spends her life in her blimp—

SCARY MUSIC

—constantly in motion, hundreds of metres in the air.

"I've been in Winnipeg for a few days. I like to watch Confusion Corner. Citizens seem sooooo stupid." Now *that's* an easy sentence to hiss.

"Track down the O'Kaye boy," she goes on. "Use all your time and energy. Even if it takes you away from *Goodlitewow!*"

"You want to put *Goodlitewow!* aside for now?"

"No, I still believe in *Goodlitewow!* But find that boy!"

(Don't worry about *Goodlitewow!* I'll tell you about it in a minute.)

"I have his address. The birthday party was at his father's condominium here in Vancouver."

"Good. Very good."

"What do you want me to do to him, Boss?"

Another shudder. The Guy Fawkes mask slips. Of course, there is no face behind it.

"For now, watch him."

For now. Yikes. This would be a good time for the scary music.

CHAPTER 7

ARCHIE MAKES A MISTAKE

Archie and his mom are in their hotel room. He's watching a *Squid Central* rerun. She's reading a best-seller about a lonely man who wants a friend. She sighs. "I'd be your friend, Arthur," she murmurs. "I need a friend too."

"And I'd be your friend, Maeve," I say. "I'd even change my name to Arthur."

She doesn't hear me. Of course. I'm telling the story. I'm in a different world.

The telephone call startles Maeve out of her Arthur dream. She picks up and listens for a moment. When she puts the phone back she frowns slightly, causing the cutest little wrinkle to appear between her eyebrows.

"That was the front desk, Arch," she says. "The Boredom Institute called the hotel on our behalf. We've been upgraded to a suite, and there's a welcome package waiting for us."

"Cool."

"They asked if either of us wanted a massage. Do you want a massage, Archie?"

"Massage? Call that a welcome package — some stranger squeezing my back? Eww. Why would I want that?"

"I wonder why we're suddenly so important? What happened to you at the Boredom Institute?"

"I don't remember anything." And he doesn't. Archie has no memory of what happens to him. He remembers being scared, but his superpower is a mystery.

"Nothing?"

"Just the usual dumb tests. And the mice." He shivers. "I hope the welcome package has peanuts in it."

"Well, I'm curious about our upgrade. Aren't you curious at all, Arch?"

"No. I like peanuts. I'm hungry." He goes back to the TV.

They spend a luxurious night in their suite. Archie eats all the nuts in the welcome package. Maeve enjoys the fruit and cheese, and packs the magazine in her carry-on bag. Next morning a stretch limousine arrives to take them to the airport.

"We look forward to seeing you again," says the lady at the front desk.

"Thank you," says Maeve. Archie is trying to make the Vulcan greeting with both hands.

☆ ☆ ☆

Because of the time change, they arrive in Vancouver only an hour or so after they take off from Montreal.

"Do I have to go to school today?" Archie asks.

His mom wants to be fair. "Why wouldn't you go?"

"Because . . . it was my birthday last week? And I was in Montreal? And I'm tired?"

"Those don't seem like great reasons to stay home. Come on, I'll drive you."

"What about lunch?"

"We ate on the plane, remember? Get your books together, Arch."

Pendrell Public is a crowded, rundown building a few blocks from their apartment. Archie arrives near the end of lunch recess. He feels grumpy, and because he's grumpy he does something stupid.

We've all made stupid mistakes, right? This morning my bathroom scale showed I had put on two pounds. Blugh! I was so grumpy I deliberately sat down and ate a gigantic bowl of cereal with brown sugar, and three pieces of toast with peanut butter, and a multigrain-nut-raisin-date-carrot-coconut-caramel-chocolate-chip muffin the size of my head. I sure didn't need all that food, but I was mad at my scale. Stupid scale, you think I've gained weight? I'll show you how to put on weight! Now I feel sleepy and I have a stomach ache.

Archie's mistake is even bigger than mine.

As usual, the big kids are playing soccer, and one of them kicks the ball out of bounds. It rolls toward Archie. Without thinking, because he's grumpy, he picks up the ball and kicks it hard. It doesn't go far, but it goes high. It ends up on the school roof.

This is bad for Archie. There are a dozen soccer players who are mad at him for ending their game, and one of them is Big Mean Ehsin. Yes, that's his name. He answers to it. If you say, "Hi there, Big Mean Ehsin," he will say "Hi" back — or maybe he'll push you down. They don't call him Big Mean Ehsin as a joke — you know, the way Robin Hood's friend Little John is not little at all. Ehsin really is big and mean.

Now he's running toward Archie, yelling and waving his large fists. There's a school rule about fighting on the playground, but Big Mean Ehsin doesn't follow rules very closely. He gets suspended a lot.

Oh dear! thinks Archie.

There are two kinds of bullies. Guy bullies, I mean. Girl bullies are different. In fact, girls and guys are different in a lot of ways. (You probably know that already.)

Of the two kinds of guy bullies, one of them is mean and slow. He's kind of pathetic. If he weren't kicking you right now, or bending your arm up behind your back, or throwing your geography project in the garbage, you might feel sorry for him.

The other kind of guy bully is mean too. All bullies are mean. But this guy is mean and fast. Him you don't feel sorry for. Him you stay away from. Big Mean Ehsin is this kind of bully. Mostly, Archie has stayed away from him. Until now.

Oh dear, Archie thinks, running as fast as his

short legs will take him, scanning the playground for help — the teacher, a friend, anyone! *Oh dear, oh dear*, he thinks. *Ehsin will catch me in a few seconds and turn me into soup. I can hear his footsteps. Why did I kick the ball? Oh dear, oh dear, oh dear.*

Other kids stop what they are doing and turn to look. The playground grows silent, except for Ehsin's yelling. The on-duty teacher looks over.

The main doors are on the other side of the playground. Archie's friend Uday is in front of them with one of the school's cameras on his shoulder. There's a script taped to the bottom of the camera.

"Okay, Dale, any time you're ready. Action."

He presses the record button. Dale holds up a familiar gold-wrapped candy bar and squints at the script. "This is not just any chocolate bar," she begins. "This bar is peanuts and caramel, but it is also hope. Hope for—"

"You're holding it upside down," Uday whispers.

She turns to check. "Darn," she says. Over Uday's shoulder, she sees Archie puffing across the playground with Ehsin pelting after him. "What's going on?"

Uday, turning to follow her pointing finger, keeps the camera rolling. Big Mean Ehsin is getting closer, closer. The adrenalin builds inside Archie and mixes with the reidium he absorbed as a baby. And it happens again. He stops, turns, and smiles. A wide, genuine smile.

When he sees the smile, Ehsin slows down, as if he's running through honey and his feet are sticky and hard to lift. He pants, and slows some more, and finally comes to a halt right in front of Archie.

"Ehsin!" Archie says. "The biggest and meanest Ehsin of them all! My gosh is that ... *you*? What a ... *total* pleasure to see you."

The words flow sweet and smooth. The smile stays in place. Ehsin lowers his fist and opens his mouth. "Hi," he says.

"I ... guess you're upset about the soccer ball," says Archie, with a grin. "I - gosh, I don't *know* what happened. One of those... *crazy* things, you know? I'm just so... clumsy. What can I say? I mean, *really?*"

The soccer players crowd around. They can see and hear Archie, and they react like Ehsin. They were angry, but now they are all smiling.

"That's okay," says one of them.

"Sure, no problem, Archie," says another one.

"Who wants to play soccer when we can hang out with you," says a third.

Archie holds up both hands in a push-away gesture. He shakes his head, still smiling. "Aw, you – you guys – are... *ridiculous.* Stop it!" he says.

Big Mean Ehsin reaches into his pocket and pulls out a roll of fruit candy. He offers it to Archie.

"Is that for me? Why – gosh, I guess I... *Thanks,* Ehsin. Thanks so much."

He takes a candy as the on-duty teacher comes over. Her name is Ms. Friesen. She teaches gym, and she's about as tough a teacher as the school has. She insists on respect. You have to respect the rules, the school, the teachers, each other. She doesn't like Big Mean Ehsin. She doesn't like Archie either. Neither of them is big on respect.

She wonders what Archie has done to make Ehsin mad. Serve them both right. "What's going on with you two?" she asks.

When she catches Archie's smile, she staggers. That's how powerful the impact is. She smiles back before she can help it. "Do you need anything, Archie? Is Ehsin bothering you?"

"Gosh, no, Ms. Friesen. He's offering me a candy."

"Well, of course he is. If I had a candy, I'd offer you one too."

"And I want to say — now — that I'm just … you know, so sorry … for kicking the soccer ball onto the roof. I'm *such* an idiot. You know?" He looks up at her in an admiring way. *If only I could be more like you,* he seems to be thinking.

"Is that what happened? You are funny, Archie! That's totally okay," she says.

The bell rings. Lunch is over.

As the soccer players drift toward the school doors, Archie bites down on his candy and starts to feel better. His shoulders slump, his hair musses itself, and the tail of his shirt makes its way out of his pants.

CHAPTER 8

PAKORAS AND CHERRIES AND GOODLITEWOW!

Three hours later, Archie and Dale and Uday are watching the whole scene again. They're sitting in Uday's living room. Uday took the school camera home so he could film Dale talking about Chompo again (more about that in a minute). They're watching the replay on TV. Uday can't get over it. Something weird happened on the playground. But what?

"What did you *do*, Archie?" asks Uday.

Archie shrugs and reaches for some food. Uday's nani puts out a snack as soon as her grandson comes in the door. Today it's pakoras and cherries. Archie takes a big bite. Crumbs go everywhere.

"I didn't get beat up," he whuffles. "That's the main thing. Oh, and Big Mean Ehsin gave me a candy."

"Play it again," says Dale, spitting out a cherry pit.

"Sure." Uday replays the scene.

"Stop!" Dale leans forward. "Look at Big Mean Ehsin. See the way his face just collapsed into a smile? When was the last time you saw that?"

Uday shakes his head. "Never."

"I can't see your face, but everyone is smiling," says Dale. "Even Friesen is smiling, and she hates you, Archie. What did you say?"

"I dunno. I don't remember any of it." Archie is concentrating on his pakora. Uday is trying to remember where he's seen the look on Ms. Friesen's face before.

"Friesen still talks about you refusing to do jumping jacks in gym last year. Remember?" Dale asks.

Archie shrugs and swallows. "I didn't refuse to do them. All I said was that we looked silly."

"And she made you do some by yourself, and everyone laughed, and you said, 'See what I mean.' Friesen has hated you ever since. But look at her big smile here. She reminds me of the waitress at your birthday."

"That's it!" Uday is excited. "Remember, Archie? At the end of the party? You came running in, and suddenly I thought that waitress was going to kiss you."

"Eww." Archie has never been kissed by a girl who wasn't family. Or a guy for that matter. He figures kissing is yucky. "I don't remember that at all," he says.

"Friesen is looking at you the same way," says Uday. "Imagine getting everyone to like you! How did you do that?" He steals an adoring look at Dale.

Dale can't understand what's going on in the video. She knows why *she* likes Archie. He comes out with whatever he's thinking about. Often a real weird idea. He surprises her into laughter. But she understands why most people think he's a dork. What would make a guy like Big Mean Ehsin — a bully — suddenly smile and offer him candy? It was a mystery.

Candy. That reminds her. "While you have the camera here, Uday, can we try that Chompo bar ad again? I have the script in my purse. Archie can hold it for me to read while you shoot."

"We'll shoot later," Uday says. He means when Archie isn't there and it's just the two of them. "I'll hold the script. Archie doesn't care about the homeless like I do."

"Don't you, Archie?"

"Eh?"

"The homeless. Don't you want to help them?"

"How? I'm not going to give them my home."

"Come on, Archie!"

Uday has a little smirk on his face. "Yes, that's right. Come on, Archie! Be more caring."

Uday's nani comes into the living room, carrying

a tray. "Drinks!" she says. "Who wants drinks?" Mrs. Sawnay is a small, tidy lady in a light-coloured sari. She was shopping at the market earlier today, trying to please her grandson.

"I do not know this product," she says. "The display poster was very prominent. Try, please. It is healthy for you."

She puts the tray on the coffee table. Three bottles of clear liquid. Twist-off caps. The label on each bottle shows a picture of an open mouth. Like a medical picture. You can see lips, teeth, tongue, tonsils, uvula — the whole thing. The name is in bold capital letters across the bottom of the label: *Goodlitewow!*

"Thank you," says Dale. "And thanks for the snack. The cherries were great."

Mrs. Sawnay sniffs. "I did not make the cherries."

Dale blushes. "Well, the pakoras were amazing too. Right, Archie? You ate about six of them."

"Eh?"

Mrs. Sawnay exits. Uday takes a swig of *Goodlitewow!* and screws his face up. Dale takes a small sip and puts the bottle down. "Oh," she says. That's all. She wishes there was something else to drink. But she's afraid to go into the kitchen for a glass of water, in case Mrs. Sawnay is there. Archie wishes there were more pakoras.

CHAPTER 9

CHOMPO CHOMPO

They live in the west end of Vancouver, not far from English Bay. That's where the three of them are, a half hour later. It's a cloudy afternoon, not too cold. The beach is quiet.

Uday has one foot on the sand and the other on the grass. He points the camera at Dale, who stands under a tree, holding the familiar gold-wrapped candy bar. Archie stands out of the shot, holding up a piece of paper filled with block printing.

"Any time," says Uday.

She waves away an insect, peers at the paper, clears her throat, turns toward the camera, and holds out her hand. "This," she says, "is more than a chocolate bar. Much more. It is— Archie! Stop laughing."

Now he's sputtering. Some saliva went down the wrong way when he laughed. He coughs a couple of times and clears his throat. Uday shakes his head. He knew bringing Archie was a mistake.

"Stop it. And hold my script higher," says Dale.

"Call this a script?" Archie shakes the piece of paper. "Who writes that stuff? You're holding a Chompo bar. That's exactly what it is. It's not more than a chocolate bar. It's not less than a chocolate bar. It's a chocolate bar. Sheesh."

Dale flushes. "Bounderbury Chocolate will donate twenty-five cents from every Chompo sale to build a homeless shelter. That's why—"

"I know. You told me. You and Uday and that guru, holding lotus blossoms. Why not just tell the truth? Look into the camera and say the chocolate bar tastes good. Here, I'll do it. Uday can film me. I'll eat and people will donate money. Watch." He grabs the Chompo bar out of her hand.

"Archie! Stop! This is our last chocolate bar."

"Don't be a dork!"

"This Chompo bar," he begins, with an unconvincing smile, "will taste great. Mmm-mmm good. Can't wait."

He tears off the wrapper. Takes a bite. Uday shrugs at Dale. "I guess we can shoot tomorrow."

She waves again at that passing insect. "Uday's right, Archie. You can be a real dork. Hang on."

Dale takes out her phone and stares at the name on the screen. "Mr. O'Kaye? Hello, it's Dale. Did you want to talk to Archie? He's right here. He— oh. What did you say? Oh my. That's terrible . . ." She turns to concentrate, covering her other ear, and walks away down the beach.

The insect Dale waved at is a wasp. Sensing the candy bar, it flies closer. Closer. Archie, his mouth full of chocolate and caramel, hears the wasp buzzing right in his ear, an intense vibration. You know the sound. What do you do when you hear it? That's what Archie does: he panics.

You freak out loudly and visibly when you panic, don't you? I sure do. When the smoke alarm goes off because something on the stove is burning, I scream and run around the kitchen waving towels.

Archie doesn't freak out like this. He doesn't freak out at all *on the outside.* Inside he's screaming *Oh no! Oh no! Oh no!* but outside he is as calm as an old piece of soap. The extra adrenalin works on his whole body from the vocal cords out.

And he becomes — suddenly, strangely, totally — fascinating.

It happens now, with the wasp buzzing in his ear. Archie doesn't scream or wave his arms wildly. He smiles. He looks neater and cleaner, and stands taller. His personality radiates all the way out to Beach Street, causing a passerby to drop her ice-cream cone and stare at him.

"Well, well," he says. "What do we have here?"

The sudden force of his personality hits Uday like a wave at high tide. He can't help turning toward Archie. The camera turns with him. He focuses on his friend, holding a tight shot for the next minute. Just the face and the candy bar. Archie's smile would melt glass.

"This is a Chompo," he says, holding it out in the direction of the wasp — and the camera. "Do *you*...

uh... want some? It's good. It's... really good. Here, we can share it."

Archie takes another bite. The wasp flies away. "Mmm," he says.

"I'm really sorry for what happened, Mr. O'Kaye," says Dale, who has been talking all this time. "I'll tell Archie to call you now. And I'll tell him to check his phone more often. Goodbye."

She's standing near the water. Out in the middle of the bay, a giant container ship pulls up its anchor. Dale turns to look back up the beach. Uday is filming Archie eating the chocolate bar. They both seem pretty serious. Someone is watching. It's the woman who dropped her ice cream. She's wearing a deep green skirt patterned with dragonflies. She stands next to Archie with her mouth open.

"You," she says. "I saw you. I heard you."

Archie is no longer as afraid as he was a minute ago. The wasp is gone. He comes out of his spell and looks over at the woman.

"Eh?" he says.

"Do you like Chompo bars?" she asks. "I want to buy one. I want to buy one now. Would you like that? Would you?"

Archie's hair is starting to muss a bit. His power is wearing off. He is reverting to his normal self. He shrugs elaborately, shakes his head. "I don't care what you do."

Dale runs up from the waterfront with less than her usual grace. "Archie! Archie! Phone your dad."

"Huh? Why?"

"It's important."

The woman with the dragonfly skirt looks around. "Chompo," she says. "Chompo." She wanders toward Denman Street.

Uday switches off the camera and licks his lips. He has a sudden craving too. What's going on? When he pictures Archie saying "Mmm," he wants a Chompo bar more than he has ever wanted anything. More than he wants a new phone from his parents, or a kiss from Dale. He swallows, looks around. There's a variety store on the corner. Maybe he can pick up a Chompo there.

What's with Archie? Yeah, that's him, nodding, saying, "Sure, whatever," putting away his phone, picking his nose and wiping his finger on his pants. He's the same tiresome dumb doofus Uday has put up with for the last couple of years. What got into him just now? What on earth happened?

Archie and Dale come over together. "Archie has to go home," she whispers. "Someone broke into his dad's place."

Archie sighs. "Now I have to make a list of stuff that's missing."

"It was your room they trashed," she says. "Your bedroom. Isn't that creepy, Uday?"

"Yes, most definitely. Creepy is the word. Would you like company, Archie? Dale and I would go to your father's with you."

"Nah, whatever," says Archie. "Dad's in a hurry. He told me to get a cab." He waves without looking back. A couple of tourists are getting out of a taxi. He pushes past them, slides into the back seat, and slams the door.

Uday walks Dale to her bus stop. They stop at the

variety store, but there are no Chompo bars on the shelf. Dale points out the display for *Goodlitewow!* Uday grimaces instinctively at the memory of the taste. The old guy behind the counter notices them.

"You want to buy?" he asks. "You want *Goodlitewow!* I'll give you half price."

Uday shakes his head. "I want a Chompo."

"Chompo! You too! What's going on here? A woman just came in and bought all my Chompo bars. A box of twenty-four. Plus the bars on display. Never seen that before, and I been in this business a long time."

Uday still wants a Chompo. He wonders. It's a crazy idea, but . . . "You didn't see Archie eat the candy bar, did you?" he asks Dale, when they head out of the store.

"You mean back at the beach? I was talking to his dad."

"So you didn't see or hear him."

"No."

"I filmed it, you know. Him eating the Chompo bar."

The lights changes, and they cross Denman at Davie. The sun breaks through the cloud bank behind them. English Bay turns silver.

"Do you really want to make money for the homeless shelter?" he asks Dale.

"Oh yes."

"I'll send you a link tonight. Tell me what you think."

Her bus comes. He walks up the Davie hill, following his own shadow. He'll upload Archie's video when he gets home. But maybe he'll stop at a variety store on the way. He still really wants a Chompo bar.

CHAPTER 10

THE MAP ON THE WALL

Archie spends an hour in his dad's place, talking to a police officer and a man from the insurance office. The condo is a mess. Drawers open, floor covered with toys and clothes and books and bowls, furniture tossed around. Walking across the living-room floor makes a crunching sound.

Mr. O'Kaye is shocked and upset. His shoulders shake. "It's an invasion, man," he says, holding up a sofa cushion with the stuffing coming out. "That's what it is, an invasion!" He makes it sound like D-Day.

The police officer shrugs. She's seen worse. "TV is still here," she says. "And the other electronics. These weren't junkies looking for stuff they could sell quick. Whoever it was, looks like they were hunting for something in particular. You sure you're not missing something, Mr. O'Kaye? Something valuable — jewellery, artwork, a coin collection?"

"I don't have anything like that."

"What about you, kid? They spent a lot of time in your room."

The officer is taller than Archie, and wider. She has thick eyebrows. She leads him around the corner to the small second bedroom. "This your room, eh? They went over it pretty good." She puts her hand on his shoulder, talks quietly. "Your dad's not here, kid. It's just you and me. I want to be sure. I understand you spend time here and at your mom's. That right?"

Archie nods.

"And I guess you have a stash somewhere, eh? Secret stuff. Toys or money. Love notes from your girlfriend. That kind of thing. Hmmm?" She raises the eyebrows.

Archie shrugs. "I don't know. I keep gummi worms in my desk drawer. Hey, there they are! Cool." He bends to pick up the package. "Geez. Call this a burglary? These guys didn't take anything important at all."

"Nothing? Are you sure? What about there?" She points at a bare picture hook.

Archie looks blank.

"They made a big mess but didn't take much. There's

a photo missing from your dad's wall. Did you have one too? What used to hang there?"

Archie frowns. Let's see. The big bright *Squid Central* poster is still over the bed. The picture that Dale gave him — the Buddha sitting cross-legged with his hand out like he's flipping you the bird — is by the door. He can't remember what hung over the desk. The room is a real mess. That Buddha seems the only calm thing.

His hand gesture is called a mudra, by the way. It could look a bit rude to some, but it's not meant to. Buddha's face is full of acceptance and wisdom. And the mudra inspires Archie.

"I remember now — there was a map on the wall," he tells the cop. "That's all. An old map. Not worth anything."

They walk back to the living room. Archie's dad and the insurance guy have found two dining-room chairs to sit on. They are going over the list of damaged items.

Archie fishes a remote from the mess on the floor, sets up a chair in front of the big-screen TV, and turns it on. "Still works," he says.

He settles in to watch whatever's on. News in English? No. In French? No. Punjabi? No. *Smurfs* rerun? Sure. Archie sits back into the chair.

The police officer leaves her card with Mr. O'Kaye and heads back to the station to fill out her report.

"Will you get the stuff back?" Archie's dad calls after her.

"We'll try, sir. But I wouldn't hope too hard."

Archie smiles at Papa Smurf yelling at Brainy.

Meanwhile . . .

CHAPTER 11

THE GOOD GUYS?

The image on the computer screen wears a Lone Ranger mask, which is a little weird because there is nothing around or behind the mask. Clementine Clutterbucket can see the narrow elastic band holding the mask onto her boss's head.

That's right, we're back with the villains. Clementine and her boss, the former Nurse Nussbaum, are hashing out the *Goodlitewow!* campaign. I told you I'd fill you in.

"Why are sales so low?" hisses The Boss.

Funny that I call them the villains. Actually, I feel sorry for them. Clementine is a loyal person, trying to help her boss. And Nurse Nussbaum is a victim. Thirteen years ago she was in love with Dr. Fassbinder.

He left her behind, and after she turned invisible, he said, *I thiiinnk we shooouuld see other peeeeople. Especially since I cawn't see yooooou.* She felt sad and angry. These are normal feelings. If someone is mean to you, you want to hurt them, don't you? Even if you still like them.

So I can't blame The Boss for wanting revenge on the four children — Fassbinder's reidium experiments. He cares about them more than her. If she uses them, or destroys them, that will hurt the doctor. No, I don't blame her. But in this story she and Clementine are the bad guys. They are working against Archie, and he is our hero. Whatever that means. Heroes, villains — they're just words. They change places when you change point of view. Everyone thinks they are the good guys.

This scene takes place in Clementine's basement down on 66th Street, about the time Archie got out of school. They are talking about *Goodlitewow!* Clementine is in charge of sales and marketing for the business empire.

"Why are sales so low?" hisses the Boss.

"I have the Canada-wide survey results here. Focus groups are consistent."

"Our research is good. We know what people want. We tell them *Goodlitewow!* clears skin blemishes, grows hair, whitens teeth, improves posture, gives you energy and takes weight off. What do people say to that?"

Clementine looks down at the sheets in front of her. "Everybody says it tastes terrible, Boss," she says.

"Everybody?" (Can you hiss that word? I really don't know how she does it.)

"Well, everybody we surveyed."

Here's the report.

RATING THE FLAVOUR OF GOODLITEWOW!
RESPONDENTS' RESULTS ARE ROUNDED TO NEAREST PERCENTAGE.

1)	MAGICALLY DELICIOUS	0%
2)	EXCELLENT	0%
3)	VERY GOOD	0%
4)	PRETTY DARN GOOD	0%
5)	NOT BAD	0%
6)	MEH	0%
7)	I'VE HAD WORSE	0%
8)	KIND OF LOUSY	0%
9)	REALLY QUITE UNPLEASANT	7%
10)	DOWNRIGHT AWFUL	34%
11)	WORST. TASTE. EVER.	59%

The Lone Ranger mask looks left, looks right. The invisible Boss is shaking her head.

"What is wrong with people?" says Clementine. "The flavours they don't like are the best ones."

(Remember, this is the woman who shops for sneeze-weed and mugwort.) "Garlic? Cough syrup? Skunk?" she says. "Mmm, mmm, amazing! Who doesn't like the smell of fresh skunk?"

"What should we do now?" The Boss asks. "You're my marketing guru. Should we test the other flavour mixes? There was one with dill pickle, I recall."

Clementine consults her file. "That's right, Boss. Good memory. We had three to choose from: skunk–cough syrup, dill pickle–nutmeg and tuna fish–espresso."

The Boss sighs — a long escape of air. She sounds like a tire going slowly flat. "I try to make people feel better about themselves," she hisses. "But they don't *want* to be helped. It's a sick world we live in, Clutter-bucket. A sick and lazy world."

"Yes, Boss."

A loud banging and hooting comes from the downstairs of Clementine's apartment. She listens for a moment, nodding when she recognizes one of the voices. "My henchpeople have returned from the O'Kaye place," she says.

"Is he the right O'Kaye?"

"I'll let you know as soon as I find out, Boss."

CHAPTER 12

CALL THAT A LOOK?

Back to our hero. Archie is leaning into the fridge at his mom's. He'll be staying at her place until his dad cleans up after the burglary. Archie's upset because the fridge is empty except for stuff like red peppers and apples and pomegranate juice. Which he does not like. He slams the door and pouts.

"Geez, isn't there *anything* good to eat?"

"Actually, I thought we could order pizza. How's that, Arch?" his mom calls from the bathroom. She's putting on makeup.

"Good. And brownies and a six-pack of Mountain Dew. Pizza Mansion has a special."

"Sure," his mom replies, her voice muffled by the Kleenex she uses to blot her lipstick. She's getting ready for a date. She's distracted. Maybe that's why she goes along with Archie's ideas for dinner. This is her first date in a while. She deserves to have some fun. I hope things work out for her.

Archie settles into the big chair in the living room and un-pauses *Gang of Greats*. His avatar is a Third-Level Spellcaster who has just put a Gorg to sleep. He reaches out to steal its flaming sword. But he's too slow. The sleeping spell turns the Gorg into triplets, all with flaming swords. Oops! Time to turn invisible — or run — or both.

Maeve calls Pizza Mansion as she heads to the bedroom to choose her outfit. "Hello! I'd like to order a medium pizza with pepperoni and sausage and bacon and green pepper."

"Ma! No pepper!"

"Sorry," she says into the phone. "Cancel the pepper. I was just trying to get a vegetable into my son."

Twenty minutes later there's a knock on the door. Maeve runs to answer it. Archie looks up with interest, but it's not the pizza. He returns to the game.

A bearded hipster in a tight vest and long leather shoes wanders into the living room behind Maeve.

"Hey, Arch, this is Cory. We're going to the symphony concert."

"Uh-huh."

Maeve tries again: "Pizza money is on the table, honey! See you later. Hey, before I go, what do you think of my outfit?" Not that she cares about her son's opinion of her clothes. But she wants him to be polite to her guest. "Do I look nice?" She twirls in the hallway. Archie glances over.

"Nope."

Cory shakes his head and sighs. "Come on, dude. Be positive. Turn the frown upside down. Can't you say something complimentary about your mom's clothes? *Anything?*" He emphasizes the last word, making it a joke.

"Weeeell, I guess her outfit looks better than *yours.*"

"Arch! Please!"

"What? Skinny pants and a vest with flowers on it? Call that a look? I guess everything else is in the wash."

Cory's laughter is a little forced. He pulls Maeve through the door. Archie goes back to the game.

Between you and me, I'm on his side. Cory seems like a weasel. I don't know what's going to happen with Cory and Maeve, but she can do better than this guy. Way better.

Meanwhile . . .

The cell tower near Neepawa, Manitoba, beams its signal to the tattered, saggy blimp.

SCARY MUSIC

"Good news, Boss," says Clementine Clutterbucket. "My agents broke into the O'Kaye condominium on 12th Street. A boy named Archie lives there. He had a birthday last week. On the bedroom wall was a map of Dimly, Manitoba. In the wall socket was a night light from Dimly Bulb."

"Ahhhhh," hisses The Boss.

"So this Archie O'Kaye was born thirteen years ago and has a connection to Dimly. He has to be the right one."

"Well done."

Today The Boss is wearing a Groucho Marx mask, glasses and a nose and moustache. The ear pieces hook onto nothing.

"Archie just had his regular tests at the Boredom Institute," says The Boss. "The others show evidence of developing power. Archie may not develop at all. But everyone agrees that he is the nicest of the four."

"I see." *Everyone*? thinks Clementine. Who is *everyone*? How does The Boss know so much about what's going on in Fassbinder's office? Does she have a source?

"Now that you know where he lives, follow him. Catch him!"

"Yes, Boss."

"The moment he shows any gift, let me know."

"Yes, Boss."

"Meanwhile, devote yourself to *Goodlitewow!*"

"Yes, Boss."

The computer screen, with its unfunny glasses, false nose and moustache, goes dark.

Later that night, Archie is getting ready for bed, splashing his face with lukewarm water and rubbing his toothbrush over his teeth. His mom still isn't home. Maybe she died of boredom, hanging out with that guy at a concert. A case for Sherlock Holmes, he thinks. *There are no clues. The corpse has not a mark on her, but her face bears a look of horrible suffering, as the symphony claims another victim. Classical music is dangerous!*

Archie's phone buzzes as he gets into bed. It's a text from Uday: "Check this out!"

Archie opens the link. It's the joke ad he did that afternoon down at English Bay. Uday must have uploaded it. Archie watches himself eat a Chompo bar and say "Mmmmm." That's it. That's the link. All of thirty seconds?

He texts back: "So what?"

The reply surprises him: "Amazing! You are absolutely amazing. I've sent it to everyone!" He never thought Uday admired him. He shrugs. Whatever.

A few minutes later he hears his mom coming home from her date. Alone. Which is a relief. He's not jealous, but if she's with Cory she won't pay as much attention to him. I guess that's a kind of jealousy.

She checks on him, standing in the half-open doorway of his bedroom.

"Have you seen my night light?" Archie asks. "I don't want to sleep in the dark."

"Is it at your dad's?"

"Maybe. I didn't see it when I was packing."

"Do you really still need that thing, Arch?"

"Uh-huh."

The hall light shining behind her makes her look like a shadow. She doesn't move away — she wants to talk. "So, how was *your* evening?"

"Fine."

She waits for him to ask her about her evening. But he doesn't. Come on, Archie! Nope.

"Want to know how my date went?" she asks, finally.

"Eh? No."

"Because it was fun."

"Still no," he says.

She smiles and moves away.

I have to say I'm surprised her date went well. I didn't think much of Cory. I guess I was wrong. Maybe he is the right guy for Maeve. And it might do Archie good to have another adult around. Maeve lets him get away with a lot. Tonight she lets him leave the door half-open and the hall light on. My mom never let me do that when I was scared of the dark.

CHAPTER
13

THE QUEEN BEES

An hour before school starts, the staff room of Pendrell Public is full, and silent except for rustled papers and slurped coffee. There's an emergency staff meeting! Attendance compulsory!!

Principal Susie Loewen sent a memo yesterday and reinforced it with an email last night. She likes exclamation points! How much? This much!!! There is only one item on the agenda.

1) Fire Drill!

Pendrell Public's archrival is the Haro Street Academy, a few blocks away. Last week Haro Street had a fire drill. The school emptied less than five minutes after the fire bell started to ring, and got a note from the Vancouver Fire Department praising them for the speedy exit. The Haro principal, Carol Rempel, has been bragging ever since. Principal Loewen wants Pendrell to do better.

Yes, fire drills are supposed to be a surprise. And yes, fire drills are about safety, not speed. Principal Loewen knows this. But she can't *stand* the thought of Carol Rempel crowing about that letter from the VFD for the next six months.

"We have to get our kids out faster," she says to the staff. "We have to!" Loewen is an intense individual, as thin as a bundle of sticks. She grips the edge of the table. Her hair hangs in a smooth combed waterfall. Fire comes out of her eyes. "I don't know exactly when the drill begins," she says. "But it'll be this afternoon. Keep your classes alert! Monitor bathroom use. Okay, that's it. Meeting over."

She stalks back to her office with catlike intensity. Every step perfectly placed. The teachers shrug at each other. *That Loewen is kind of crazy, eh?*

Ms. Zabriskie, the grade seven teacher, is halfway through a Chompo bar. It's her second one this meeting. "I don't know what it is," she says, "but ever since I saw the video my student sent me, I feel like I have to support the project."

"Huh?" asks her neighbour, who is gathering up his papers. "What project?"

"I'll send you the link," says Ms. Zabriskie. "I've already sent it to a bunch of people."

Of course, the video is Archie eating the Chompo bar. Uday sent it to Dale, who couldn't open it but forwarded it to everyone on her contact list.

While the teachers are meeting, Archie is yawning his way through breakfast. His mom leaves for work halfway through, with an extra little bounce in her step.

Archie slouches down Pendrell Street alone and yawning. The school bell rings as he enters the playground.

He is in front of his locker collecting his books when Wilhelmina comes over with Roxy and Kristina. These are the class Queen Bees. Most of the other girls want to be their friends, even after Wilhelmina has made fun of them. Most of the guys would like to go out with them. All year these three have ignored Archie. Today they stand in a circle around him, smiling.

"Hellooooo," says Wilhelmina, with the dark hair and wide-set green eyes.

"Hi, Archie boy," says Roxy, with the blond curls, cheekbones and light brown skin.

"Hey, hey, Archie," says Kristina, with the braces.

He grunts. He's trying to squeeze the math book out of the bottom of the stack.

"Ready, girls?" says Willie (that's her nickname, and it's easier to spell; I'll just call her that). On her cue, they all pull Chompo bars out of their bags.

"Whaddya think, Archie boy?" Roxy's cheekbones stick out like a hockey player's elbows.

Archie gives up trying to save time. He heaves all the books out, takes the math book, and throws the rest back in the locker. "Eh?" he says. "What do I think? I think it's a school day and I didn't get enough sleep. And I have a new pimple on my forehead." When he turns around and the girls actually see him for the first time today, they blink and shake their heads. It's like they are waking from a dream.

"Ew!" says Roxy. "A pimple!"

"You're . . . Why, you're just Archie," says Willie.

"Ew," says Kristina. "You're the same old loser you've always been."

Each of the three of them takes a step back at the same time. Like they are playing Simon says. Their faces are all scrunched up.

Archie yawns. "Man, am I bored," he says, kicking his locker shut and walking away.

The three girls huddle together. "He looked different in the video," whispers Kristina.

"Lighting, probably," says Roxy.

"Camera magic," says Willie.

Other girls follow the Queen Bees around. Does this happen at your school? "Hey! You guys are all eating Chompo bars," says one of them. "Look! I have a Chompo too. I bought it on the way to school. Hey, I'm just like you guys!" She pulls a bar from her pocket.

"Not with those pants you're not, Sage," says Willie, shaking her head. Roxy and Kristina look at each other. Chocolate sprays from their mouths when they snicker.

"What? What's wrong with my pants? They're new."

"Yes, Sage. Yes, they are." Willie's smile gets wider and meaner until it turns into a genuine smirk. The other girls — the hangers-on — start to laugh. They don't know why, but they do it. Willie's laughing, so there must be something wrong with Sage's pants. Willie shops on Alberni Street. (Actually, Willie is just a meanie. She likes the feeling of power she gets when less popular girls squirm.)

"Ha, ha, ha." Sage laughs along with the rest, trying to be a good sport, trying not to show how puzzled and hurt she is.

The morning passes slowly and weirdly at Pendrell Public. Sudden noises make the teachers go off like popcorn.

"Are you all right, Ms. Zabriskie?" Dale asks at the end of math class. "You seem awfully jumpy today."

"I am a little stressed."

"You should try to relax. Do you ever do any breathing exercises? We do one in yoga, and it really works! I use it all the time."

Ms. Zabriskie is expecting the fire alarm. The principal wants them all to move fast. It could happen at any time today. Any time at all.

"What you do," says Dale, "is breathe *in* energy, and breathe *out* where you want the energy to go. Isn't that wonderful? If I'm exercising, I breathe in energy and breathe out to my arms and legs. If I'm doing homework, I breathe in energy and breathe out to my—"

The bell rings, and Ms. Zabriskie leaps a foot.

Next period is geography. Dale follows Sage down the hall. "Hey, I like your pants," she says. "Are they new?"

The smaller girl turns with a look of desperate fury. "Yes!" she shouts. "Yes, they are new! Very new! I'll never wear new pants again!" She stomps away.

Wow, thinks Dale. *Sounds like someone could use a breathing exercise.*

She and Uday sit at their usual cafeteria table for lunch. "Have you been checking YouTube?" he says. "Fifty thousand hits in less than a day! Trending for hours. Look at the comments! It's on Reddit and BuzzFeed and Facebook and Spezzlow. Holy cow! It's viral!" He holds up his phone. The hit counter on the Chompo clip counts like a stopwatch.

"I sent it to everyone," he says. "But I never thought this would happen. Remember how we were going to shoot you making the same pitch? No point to that. We'll never get more attention than this! I have an idea. Let's wait until Archie gets here." He takes a bite of his lunch. Spring rolls today. Nani makes them Vietnamese-style. So tasty.

Dale looks thoughtful. "Are you making fun of religion?" she asks.

"Huh?"

"When you say holy cow, are you poking fun at Hinduism? You were born Hindu, so maybe that's okay. I believe we should be kind to all creatures — that is the true religion. What? What are you staring at?"

"Nothing."

"Did I sound too earnest? I did, didn't I? I heard it. Sorry. I can't help myself. If you want to laugh at me, go ahead. Archie does."

Uday sees a chance. "I'll never laugh at you," he says. "I'm a real friend. You can trust what I say. Not like Archie."

Dale considers this while she unwraps her lunch. "Archie doesn't always say nice things. But he's sincere. He says what he thinks."

She's right. Even if Archie doesn't think very hard. Or seriously. Or often.

"So do I. What do you have today? Those look like bhajis." He takes one.

"They are bhajis. I made them myself from Neil Flambé's recipe."

"They taste . . . wonderful." Uday smiles and swallows with difficulty.

CHAPTER 14

HOLY COW!

55,789 HITS

Archie is late for lunch. He slumps into a chair beside Uday. "People are weird," he says. "Stopping me in the hall, grabbing my shirt. Took me forever to get here from science class." He takes one of Uday's spring rolls and throws his own lunch on the table. The three of them share everything.

"Hey, these are good," he says with his mouth full. "I wish my nana cooked like your nani. Who wants a turkey sandwich?"

"Me," says Dale.

Two girls from another grade seven class come over to their table. They're shy and giggly. One of them wears a beret. The other has a whole stitch of earrings going down the outside of her left ear.

"We love your video, Archie," they say together.

"You know, I shot that video," says Uday, sitting up straight, smiling right at the one with the beret. "And edited it. Uploaded it myself."

The girls ignore him, edge closer to Archie. "Do you have any Chompo bars for us?" asks the one in the beret. (Her name is Violet. Her friend is Kelly. They aren't important to the story. In fact, this is the only scene they are in. So you don't have to remember them.)

"No," says Archie. "If I did, I'd eat it myself."

"Wow. You're mean," says Kelly.

"And you're magnetic."

"Huh?"

"If I had a magnet right now, it would go right for your earrings. Magnetic. See?" Archie collapses in giggles.

"Archie! That was rude." Dale doesn't think Kelly is very nice, but there is such a thing as manners. "Sorry," she calls after the girls, who are already on their way back to their own table.

Archie takes a bite from one of Dale's bhajis. Uday's nani packed him a bottle of *Goodlitewow!* but no one wants it. It sits on the table, unopened.

"I've been thinking," Uday says. "We have to talk, guys. Look around the cafeteria. I can count twelve Chompo bars. That is twelve more than I noticed yesterday. The candy machine in the lobby is out of the bars. This has happened in one day, and all of it has to do with that video. What is going on?"

Archie shakes his head. Uday shows him the phone. "Holy cow, 55,789 hits!" Uday says. "I sent the link to fifty people. Think of all the forwarding and reforwarding. Why? Archie, why do people *believe* you? Why do they want to buy this chocolate bar just because you say so? Even I want to buy the chocolate bar, and I know what a *badir* you are. How do you do it? How do you convince tens of thousands of people, Archie? Archie!"

"Eh? What? What?" Archie's screwing his eyes closed, pinching his lips, shaking his head. "*These* are awful." He puts down the unfinished bhaji and uncaps the *Goodlitewow!* Remember, he didn't try it at Uday's place yesterday. This is his first taste. "*Gaah!* That's even worse!"

"Archie! I made those bhajis."

He shudders. The aftertaste of *Goodlitewow!* brings out the hint of skunk. "Do you like them?"

Dale has to smile. "Actually, no. But Uday does."

"Can we get back to the video?" says Uday. "How do you become so darned irresistible, Archie? How do you convince—" he checks his phone "—55,800 people to watch you?"

"Where do you get fifty-five thousand? You just said you only sent my link to fifty people."

Uday sighs. "Sixty thousand hits means tens of thousands of people watching, not fifty people watching it a thousand times each."

Archie explodes in laughter. "A thousand times. Wow. It would take all day. Call that a life! But I still don't understand."

The vice-principal steps through the cafeteria doors, spots our trio of pals, and hurries over. "You're Archie O'Kaye," he says. "You're supposed to have a detention tonight for not standing up for 'O Canada.' But after Ms. Zabriskie sent me the link to your video, I'm cancelling the detention. You don't have to stay late."

"Eh?" says Archie.

"Good work, young man. I'm impressed at your improvement. You take things more seriously than before."

The VP takes a Chompo bar out of his pocket. "My lunch," he says. "And I know that when I eat it, I'm helping a good cause." He walks off.

Uday punches Archie in the shoulder. "That's what I'm talking about," he says. "That's what's so cool!"

"I still don't get it," says Archie. "So a lot of people see the clip and buy Chompo bars. And Dale's — whatever it is — yoga studio, bird sanctuary . . ."

"Homeless shelter," she says. "Geez, Archie! Homeless shelter! And it's not mine. It belongs to the people who will live and work there." She takes an angry bite of pear.

"Whatever. So your homeless shelter gets money from the chocolate company. What's your idea, Uday? Why do you look like you're about to pee your pants?"

Uday leans over the table, talks quietly and intensely: "Can you do it again, Archie? Can I film a clip of you promoting something else?"

"Why?"

"So we can make money too."

An hour later, Archie is in gym class with Mr. Burton. Gymnastics. Horse, parallel bars, rings. Gym is not Archie's favourite class. In red shorts and a white T-shirt that are both too big for him, he looks like a limp Canadian flag. Today is an especially bad day. He tries to vault over the horse and falls to the side. He tries to swing on the parallel bars and falls between them. He climbs up the ladder to grab on to the rings, then twists himself around. Somehow his foot gets caught. He can't pull it out. He's stuck, mostly upside down, swinging gently back and forth, when the bell rings. Not the period bell. The fire-alarm bell.

Mr. Burton knows how important the fire drill is. The principal made it very clear at this morning's meeting. As soon as the bell starts, he unlocks the gym's big side doors. They open directly onto the playground.

"Okay, people!" he shouts. "Get out of here. Stand in rows on the playground. Go, go, go! Every second counts."

"Hey!" yells Archie.

The gym is full of noise. No one hears him. People are shrieking and running. Ten seconds pass. Twenty. Thirty. A minute.

"Hey!" Archie is five metres in the air, upside down. His leg is stuck through one of the rings. He is helpless. He starts to panic.

CHAPTER
15

WHAT ABOUT MAEVE?

I hate to leave Archie hanging there, but nothing bad will happen to him. Let's check in on his mom.

Maeve is on her lunch break. She works at Science World, arranging programs that kids will enjoy, usually involving bugs and snakes and poison and stuff like that. She used to bring home cockroaches and pythons for Archie to play with. Isn't that cool? (I wonder if it's why he's so scared around animals now.)

Anyway, Maeve is sitting on a bench on the seawall, eating, while she talks to Cory on the phone. Cory's her date from last night. Remember Archie made fun of his clothes? That guy. He works in event management, producing home shows and garden shows around the country.

(Don't ask me what "producing home shows" means. I don't know. He phones people who sell things like paint and aluminum siding and swimming pools and fridges, and invites them to the next show in Toronto or Minneapolis. Money is part of it, but I don't know who pays who. Does this help you understand? Not much, eh. Sorry I can't do better.)

Maeve is eating macaroni and cheese from a plastic container. She swallows some now. "I had a great time with you, Cory," she says. "Did you have fun too?"

"Oh. Uhhh, sure."

"So, do you want to go out with me again sometime soon?"

"Gee, Maeve, I . . . uh . . . I don't know about that," he says. "Maybe not too . . . soon."

It's a sparkly sunny day outside, but clouds are gathering across the horizon of her mind.

"I've been thinking, Maeve. About you and . . . Well, you and me. And the fact is— The thing's . . . well . . . The thing is that I'm going to be busy for the next little while."

"I see," she says. "Well, thanks for doing this over the phone instead of texting. That tells me something."

"I mean . . . I have events all over the—"

"And you don't have to tell me anything more. Goodbye, Cory."

She clicks her phone off, surprised to find tears in her eyes.

Don't give up, Maeve! Be open-minded. Be open-hearted. You'll see. There's someone out there for you. It could be anyone. (Anyone except Cory, that is.)

Are there are any rules in love? Take a second and think about that. It doesn't matter who you like, does it? Can you love someone whose skin is a different colour than yours? Of course you can. Who speaks a different language? Who prays like you, or not like you, or not at all? Sure. Boys or girls? Duh. People are people. Love is love. I wonder how many boundaries love can cross? I wonder.

Shoot! I forgot about Archie. Let's get back.

CHAPTER 16

FIRE DRILL HERO!

I told you nothing bad would happen to Archie, hanging from one of the rings. He's not hurt or anything. But things get tricky for a little while.

A fire engine roars up to Pendrell Public, sirens blaring. One, two, six firefighters pour out of the pumper truck and start to check around the school. Students and teachers file out of the building and line up on the playground. Principal Loewen holds a stopwatch.

"I started this watch as soon as the fire alarm sounded," she says to Captain Kenny, who stands beside her. He's in charge of the firefighting team. When the whole school is out, Ms. Loewen clicks the watch to stop it. "I make the time four minutes and thirty-three seconds from start to finish," she says.

The captain examines the watch. He has a long, horsey face and a moustache. "I think that's a record," he says.

The principal beams. A record. *Take that, Haro Academy!*

Uday and Dale stand with their science class on the playground. The fire alarm stopped ringing a while ago. They can see the principal clearly. She looks as pleased as a new grandma. Until she hears a shout over by the gym.

"Captain! Captain! Wait! Over here!"

Captain Kenny hurries over. Principal Loewen puts her watch in her purse. Her face sets like cement.

Rumour travels around the playground at the speed of gossip. In less than a minute, everyone knows what's going on.

The firefighters have found some kid trapped in the gym. The fire drill is taking a long time and Ms. Loewen is angry.

Some kid? Which kid?

"D'you think it's that guy who said you were a geeeenius?" calls someone in a clear voice. "Do you think it's him, Daisy?"

Uday and Dale look over at the new girl holding a sketchbook, and then at each other.

"Could it be Archie?" asks Uday.

Dale is tall enough to see over most of the other students' heads. "He's not on the playground," she says.

Of course it's Archie. A couple of firefighters move a box horse and ladder over to where he sways, grab him, and manage to pull his leg out from the ring. When they get him down to the gym floor he is trembling, barely able to stand upright. That's how afraid he is. He stares at the principal, vice-principal, gym teacher and firefighters, all of whom are very upset with him. And out bursts his smile. His reidium smile — the one that seems wider than his face and warmer than the sun.

"Oh, uh, *hello*," he says. "Thanks *so* much. I'm . . . gosh, I am just *terribly* clumsy. Is the fire drill over now? Oh dear. Oh dear. I must have put you *all* to, uh, lots of trouble. I am *such* a chucklehead." He shakes his head.

"Now *you*," he says to Captain Kenny, "are clearly a

man of action and distinction. A man in charge! May I presume to, um, compliment you on your uniform? So distinguished and yet rugged. It suits you, sir. It really does. Don't *you* think so, ma'am?" This to one of the other firefighters, a woman with shoulders like a pro linebacker. She stares at Archie with her mouth open. She seems unable to speak.

Archie spreads out his arms as if he is hugging them and thanking them and blessing them all at the same time. Are those tears in his eyes? Maybe.

"All of you have been so helpful," he says, with a catch in his voice. "I feel completely, totally safe. Yes, the Vancouver Fire Department has shown me a lot today. Thank you, thank you, thank you."

The playground is getting restless. What is going on? Where's the trapped kid?

"Quiet!" yell the teachers, one after the other. *Quiet. Quiet. Quiet.* The echoes roll across the playground. And in the quiet they all hear a sound of — Would you believe? — applause.

Applause? Yes. And cheering. The noise comes from the gym. Everyone turns to watch a small procession march through the open double doors and across the playground. Leading the procession are the principal and Captain Kenny. They clap noisily. Captain Kenny puts two fingers to his mouth and whistles loudly.

(I've always wanted to do that. But I can't. Whenever I try, I end up with a soft *whuffling* noise and spit all over my hand.)

Behind the principal and captain march the firefighters, who are also cheering. And on the shoulders of the first two firefighters, hoisted high, is Archie.

The procession stops in front of the rest of the school. Captain Kenny makes a speech. "This boy," he says, gesturing back at Archie, "is an example to us all. His appreciation of the Vancouver Fire Department, his generous acceptance of help and desire to profit from his experience, are lessons to live by. And in recognition of his public spirit today, the department will present this year's Community Outreach Award to Pendrell Public School!"

The playground bursts into cheers. It turns out

that the science teacher and some of the students can whistle through their fingers too. (I'm so envious!) Principal Loewen does a fist pump, thinking about what she'll say to Carol Rempel at Haro Academy. She starts chanting Archie's name. The firefighters shout with her: *Archie! Archie!*

And then one of the teachers starts her own chant. "Chompo!" she shouts. The school takes this up at once: *Chompo! Chompo!*

Hearing the name of the chocolate bar, one of the firefighters — the one with the linebacker shoulders — realizes that Archie is the guy from the video clip. She is so surprised she almost drops him. "Chompo!" she shouts in a voice of brass.

The playground is full of sound. Archie waves feebly. Uday turns to Dale. "What is *with* him?"

Dale knows Archie better than anyone. "He's scared," she says. "He's embarrassed. Look at him. Can't you see? He doesn't like being up there."

"But everyone loves him these days. When did he get to be King of the World?"

Archie! Chompo! Archie! Chompo! The playground goes wild.

"He's always been a scaredy cat," says Dale. "He still uses the night light he had from when he was a little kid."

HIGH UP, HEADING EAST

It's the next day and pitch dark except for a clock that reads 5:30. An alarm sounds. There's a sleepy grunt, and the alarm shuts off. A reading lamp goes on. We see we're in a bedroom. It's plainly furnished — a bed, dresser, mirror, bedside table and desk. There's a photograph on one wall. Window on another.

The blankets move, and then get pushed aside. But there's no one in the bed. All we can see is some pyjamas — vivid striped ones. Wait a minute. Who shut off the alarm and turned on the bedside lamp?

The photo on the wall is of a twinkly white guy with big round glasses and a smile under a bushy moustache. It's Dr. Fassbinder, thirteen years ago, standing in front of the Dimly General Hospital in Manitoba.

You know what he looks like from the graphic at the beginning of the book.

Now the pyjamas are moving. All by themselves. They stand up and walk. Can you guess where we are? That's right. We're inside The Boss's bedroom. The reason her window is rounded is that it is part of the outside wall of her blimp.

SCARY MUSIC

Oh yeah, forgot about the sound effect. It doesn't happen when I write "hot-air balloon," right? Right. Or "dirigible" or "zeppelin." I'll try to remember so I don't distract you.

The Boss is heading east. The picture of Fassbinder on the wall of her hot-air balloon gives us a hint of her obsession. His reidium experiments led to her own tragedy. Does she hate Fassbinder? If so, why would she have his picture on her bedroom wall? Why would there be marks — faint smears and smudges — on Fassbinder's face in the picture? The kind of marks you make with your fingers, or your lips?

Touching? Pathetic? Or simply creepy? You decide. Villains are not pure evil. Every bully is also a victim. (Did you know, for instance, that the mean girl teasing you about your haircut is scared of her big sister? Yes, she is.)

The striped pyjamas walk into the bathroom. Let's

not stay here any longer. Everyone deserves privacy. Villains live in the world just like you and me. Their day is full of the same daily stuff as ours. Does Lex Luthor cut his nails? Yep. Does the Green Goblin blow his nose? You bet. (And, yes, it comes out green.) Does Cruella de Vil use the bathroom? Oh yeah — a very classy one, probably with a Dalmatian-fur cover for the toilet seat. And so does The Boss. We have to remember this. But we don't have to hang around while she does it.

Okay, she's finished in the bathroom and is getting ready for the day. Today she opens the top drawer of her dresser, takes out an old-school goalie mask, and slips it over her head. In her dark top and slacks, The Boss looks like a leopard with its mouth open and teeth bared. And empty eye sockets.

She sits down at her computer.

Who has reached out to her since yesterday? What is going on in Pianvia? And Dimly? And the rest of the world?

Clementine Clutterbucket has sent a video clip with a message: "He could sell *Goodlitewow!*" The Boss opens the clip.

There's a scratch at the door. "Come in," she hisses.

The bedroom door swings slowly. There's a pattering of small feet on the floor. A high, squeaky voice calls a greeting. She ignores it.

Her attention is riveted on the screen. The kid in the video is amazing. Watching him eat the Chompo bar makes her want one right now. And she hates chocolate. No wonder there are already over seven million hits.

"Hey, Boss!" The squeaky voice is closer now. "I know that kid. I met him in Montreal. He's one of the Dimly squad that Fassbinder is studying. That's the O'Kaye kid."

The hockey mask swings around to face her visitor, who is now perched on the desk. The Boss's voice is even more sibilant than usual. "Archie O'Kaye?" she hisses.

"He got scared when he saw us. And then something weird happened. Yeah, that's Archie O'Kaye."

The Boss's message back to Clementine Clutterbucket goes to the point: "Find him! Take him!"

The flabby, dark dirigible turns east. The engine is
at maximum revs. It makes an unhappy high-pitched
whine — the same noise I make when I've eaten too
many doughnuts and I want to lie down.

CHAPTER 18

CHOCOLATE BAR MAN

"Is this what makes you special, Archie?"

"Eh?"

"You go to Montreal every year to check for gifted-ness, right? Is this your gift? Making people like you, and not be mad at you, and give you stuff?"

"I don't know."

"What do you think, Dale?"

"I don't see Archie's power myself. But I can't deny the results."

"Well, I see it. It's a superpower. And it's spectacular. We have to use it."

"Eh? Use what?"

"Uday, we are using it! The whole school is cheering for us out there. We've raised four million dollars!"

"Yeah, for the homeless. I mean we have to use it for us."

"Oh, Uday. Do not think greedy thoughts. What we think, we become, says the Buddha."

"Eh? I have no idea what you two are talking about. Selling chocolate bars? Call that a superpower? Flying and being strong are superpowers. But I can't see any mayor saying "The crime wave is out of control! Our city is being held to ransom by the forces of evil. This looks like a job for Chocolate Bar Man.'"

"Quiet, you three. The assembly is starting. I'll talk for a bit and introduce the marketing director from Bounderbury Chocolate, who will say a few words. You three stay put until you hear your names. Okay?"

"Yes, Ms. Loewen. Hello."

"Yes, Ms. Loewen. Hello."

"Eh? What? Oh, hi, Ms. Loewen. And who are you? Why are you carrying that big piece of cardboard? Those are weird glasses. Ouch. Stop pinching, Dale."

SILENCE

"Ladies and gentlemen, boys and girls, today is a proud day for Pendrell Public—"

Whoops! The story got away from me while I was on the phone with my landlady. I still owe her rent and Mrs. Ravioli says she's going to kick me out. If only narrators got paid more! I wish I could escape.

But where could I run where Mrs. Ravioli wouldn't find me?

Enough about me. Let's get back to the story. How much do I need to explain? Dale and Archie and Uday are talking to the principal. You got that, right? They're backstage in the auditorium, getting ready to take part in an assembly.

Thanks to Archie's video, Chompo sales over the last week are at historic highs, and growing daily. Bounderbury Chocolate has stepped up production at plants in Canada, England, Poland and China. In a few minutes our heroes will receive one of those big presentation cheques from Bounderbury Canada. Archie is right, by the way. The marketing director is wearing weird glasses with big fat frames made out of yellow plastic.

Ms. Loewen can't wait to post stories and pictures on all the social media sites she can find, including the local Board of Education's website. She smiles out at the crowded auditorium. "Ladies and gentlemen, today is a proud day . . ."

Okay, you're up to speed. The assembly starts off dull. They mostly are dull, right? Doesn't matter if they're about traffic safety or track and field or the Great War, assemblies are dull. Every now and then a guest will bring a banjo or a pet tiger, or say a Bad

Word, but mostly it's speeches that make grown-ups feel better and bore the breath out of you.

Principal Loewen talks about homeless in their city, and why a campaign to help them is a good thing, and how much the school cares. She introduces the marketing director, who says good morning, and what a wonderful thing the school is doing, and how young people today are our hope for the future, and *blah blah blah.* No one in the audience cares.

Things perk up when Uday and Archie and Dale come out to receive the oversized cheque from Bounderbury. Archie trips and people laugh.

The doors at the back of the auditorium open. In walks a scruffy gal with braids and a scruffy guy with a beard. The gal holds a camera with the logo of a TV station on the side. The guy holds a mic. It's officially interesting now. TV is cool, right? Better than speeches. The camera pans around the auditorium. The Bounderbury marketing director bounds to the front of the stage. Bounds? Yes, I said that.

"Glad you could make it!" A wide smile right into the camera. "You're just in time for a headline. I'm about to make a big announcement."

Big? It's huge!

"Students and teachers of Pendrell Public, get ready to be . . . blown away!"

The marketing director smiles into the camera and throws her arms wide. Did I say she was a woman? She is. Her name is Ms. Magnolia. She's big and boxy, with dark hair and a lot of rings and jewels. Young for such a responsible position. Older than you, of course, but younger than I am. I bet she doesn't have any problems paying the rent.

She's got a loud voice. She does not need a microphone to reach the back of the auditorium. "Tomorrow night! BC Place!" she says and pauses. "... Bounderbury Chocolate and their signature bar — Chompo — present a major concert to raise money for our homeless shelters with our emcee — the most famous guru in the world!"

She means the guy from Oprah. But his name is hard to say and Ms. Magnolia doesn't trust herself.

"And with the coolest band in Canada. Special musical guests: Union Duke!"

You know these guys. They're everywhere!

"And." Magnolia stabs at the audience with her finger, talking as loud as she can. "You. Are. All. Invited. Everyone from Pendrell Public gets a free ticket, and—" big pause "—a backstage pass to meet the band!"

The students have been getting more excited with every pause, every new statement. This is a fantastic assembly — even better than the one last year where the author said the Bad Word. Now they all stand and scream. Just what Magnolia wants. Her laptop is on the podium, connected to a big screen at the back of the stage. She had the school janitor and stage manager cue Archie's Chompo video clip before the assembly started. She has been saving the clip in case the TV guys didn't show. Now is the time, she figures. She pushes the button to start the video.

Big Mean Ehsin sits at the back, where he can throw scraps of paper at people. He doesn't care about music. He screams because it's fun. When the video clip comes on he stops screaming. And he's not the only one. *Chompo*, he thinks, as Archie's giant face smiles at him around the bite of chocolate and nuts and caramel. *Must get a Chompo.* "Got one of those bars on you?" he says to the kid beside him.

"Uh, no, Big Mean Ehsin. But I want one. Now."

"Me too."

Eleven rows up, snooty-girl Wilhelmina stops screaming too. "Ohhhh," she murmurs. "*That chocolate bar.*"

No one onstage can see the video because it's screening right overhead. What they can see is that the audience has stopped screaming. And . . . they all seem to be leaving.

"What is going on?" Dale whispers.

Uday gets it. He nudges Archie. "I have a plan," he says. "You and me after school. Want to make some money?"

Principal Loewen can't see the video — it's playing behind her. But she knows there's a problem. "Stop, everyone!" she yells into the microphone. "The assembly isn't over. Wait to be dismissed. Stay in your seats. That's an order." No one follows the order. The teachers don't want to stay seated either. They lead their classes outside. Everyone heads for the exits, shuffling slowly. A gym full of zombies. "Chompo," they murmur. "Chompo. Chompo."

Archie's video clip ends. The screen goes blank. The scruffy TV folks capture the scene — they are more interested in the audience than in the video clip. *Zombies Want Chompos* will be the soft news segment at the end of the local noon broadcast. Clemmie Clutterbucket will see it and get an idea. More on that later.

For now, the Chompo urge is powerful. Students and teachers mill around the halls and lockers, looking for money to buy the candy bar.

Mean, snooty Willie finds twenty dollars in her locker. She was going to use it to buy a few last-minute things for dance camp this weekend, but the call for Chompo is louder than the call for a new headband. She dashes down the hall, pushing rudely past the janitor, jostling the can of white paint he is using to touch up the door frames.

"Careful!" he shouts.

Uh-oh. Is it an open paint can? It is. Does it spill? It does. On Willie? Uh-huh.

She stands alone in the middle of the suddenly silent hall, staring down at her legs. Do you know what "aghast" means? Willie is aghast. You've never seen anyone so aghast.

Roxy hurries down the hall. "Going to the store now, Willie?" she calls.

Sage's locker is close by. Her smile is for an answered prayer. She steps forward, shaking her head sadly. "Oh dear. Not in those pants," she says. She will never forget the scene. Every time Willie says something mean to her from now on, she will remember and smile.

Real life almost never works like this. But a story can, when you've got an amazing narrator.

CHAPTER 19

BLETCH IS THE WORD

School is over. People are streaming out. Archie stands by the Pendrell Street entrance holding a brand-new pencil.

"Two dollars!" he calls. "Get your pencils here — only two dollars. They're good pencils!"

This is Uday's idea. He wants to use Archie's selling superpower to make money. Uday is a schemer. If he'd gone to school with Clark Kent, young Superman would be squeezing charcoal briquettes into diamonds during recess.

When she finds out about the scheme, Dale is disgusted. "Archie, if you have a power, use it for good!" she pleads.

"But making money is good," says Uday. Archie

agrees. He'll be getting half of the profits from the scheme.

Dale's backpack is covered in buttons that feature the Buddha's wisdom. Shrugging into the pack now, she spots the one that says: *If you truly loved yourself, you would never hurt another.*

I must not love myself then, she thinks. *Because right now I want to slap Archie.*

Over the next fifteen minutes, Archie approaches a hundred students and doesn't sell many pencils. Actually, he doesn't sell any. Total sales: zero pencils. Uday can't understand it. Why is Archie irresistible sometimes but not others? In the Chompo video, during the fire drill — but not now?

Here comes Big Mean Ehsin.

"You want a pencil?" Archie asks.

"Sure." He takes the pencil from Archie's outstretched hands.

"Excuse me. That will be two dollars," says Uday, hurrying over.

Big Mean Ehsin laughs heartily. "No it won't," he says. And keeps on walking.

Total sales: minus one pencil.

"Tuck in your shirt," Uday says. "And comb your hair. In the Chompo video you look neater."

Archie gives a high-pitched whinny. (I'd like to say

he gives a manly laugh but you know him pretty well by now. He's not a manly laugher.) "And *that's* why Ehsin wouldn't pay? Because I look sloppy?"

A handful of little kids wander out of the school-yard. Grade three or four. They're kicking stones at each other and practising their new swear word.

"Want a cool pencil?" yells Uday. "Archie O'Kaye is selling pencils. Show them, Arch!"

The kids nudge each other. "Go to bletch!" yells a one of the kids, a curly-haired rascal. "Bletch" is their swear word. I like it too. "Bletch!" You can use it for everything, and guess what it means, but it's not, you know, gross.

"Bletch you!" the rascal continues.

"Bletch *on* you!" pipes a skinny sniveller.

"You're full of bletch!" This from a cute moppet with baby teeth showing in a huge smile. They run away giggling.

"I'm getting bored. Let's go home," says Archie.

A white cargo van screeches to a stop in front of the school. On the side panel is a logo: *Goodlitewow!* The side door of the van slides open. Two guys climb out.

"There he is!" shouts one of them. "What should we do?"

"*Should?*" says the driver.

Uday spots a possible sale. He wanders toward the van, smiling. "Hi there! So, you guys recognize Archie?"

"Yeah," says the driver. "He was on the news. So was this school. We were sent to find him."

"You're right," says Uday. "Archie is on the video. And for only two bucks each you can buy pencils from him. You could even have your picture taken with him. If you ask me, that's what you *should* do. Of course," he goes on, "you might want to take off your masks before the photo, otherwise your family won't know it's you."

Yes, the driver and the two guys who are now on the sidewalk all wear masks made out of sheer nylons tied over their heads so that their faces are bulgy and hard to recognize. They look like they're about to rob a bank. Before Archie can count out three pencils, the thugs grab both boys and throw them in the back of the van.

"Go, Doc, go!" shouts the guy with his arms around Uday. The van takes off up Pendrell Street, toward the downtown.

Isn't this an exciting development? What'll our heroes do?

They don't do anything much to begin with. They sit quietly on the floor of the van, being themselves. Which means that Uday is curious.

"Why are you guys kidnapping us?" Uday asks. "Kidnapping is about money and we don't have any money. Our parents don't have any money. No one cares about us that much. We're not important."

They turn at Jervis Street. The sun is ahead of them and to the right. It shines through the passenger-side window and hits Uday in the face. He squints. "Wait — maybe we are important. You recognized Archie. This is about him, isn't it?" He leans over and punches Archie in the shoulder. "That's it. These guys want you. They know about your superpower!"

"Ow." Archie's legs are stretched out in front of him and he is looking at his shoes.

"Wow, gosh, thanks *so* much," he says. "I can walk from here. Thanks, uh, so much for stopping."

"No trouble at all," says the woman thug.

"None. Glad we could help," says the driver, from the far side.

Remember Archie's infectious laugh? He does it now, and the thugs catch his germs and laugh along without thinking, the way you sneeze without thinking when you catch cold. He waves and closes the van door. The light changes. The van turns left down Granville, toward the bridge.

Archie shakes his head to clear it. His hair starts to rumple. His shirt pops out of his pants. He has no memory of the last five minutes. He remember trying to sell pencils, and then — nothing. *What just happened?* he thinks. *How did I get here?*

"Superpower?" says one of the masked guys. "Did you hear that, Doc — he said superpower."

"I heard," says the driver.

Uday is excited. He was right all along. This is so cool!

Archie is thinking about what he'd rather be doing than sitting on the floor of the van. He could be playing *Gang of Greats*. He could be eating chips. He could be watching *Squid Central* on Channel 47. He could be reading the latest Flynn Goster comic.

One of the masked guys is laughing. Wait — it's not a guy, it's a girl. A woman. He didn't notice before. Now that he can hear her voice he realizes that she's a woman. She's staring down at him and laughing. He looks up. "What?"

"I like your boxers," she says. "I watch *Squid Central* too."

Archie gasps. That's right — his fly is open, and his brightly coloured underpants are clearly visible.

He zips up right away. *Now* he's feeling something. He feels pretty darn embarrassed. How long has his zipper been down? All that time he was pushing pencils outside the school? Did those sassy little kids see? Did Big Mean Ehsin? And now this woman. Oh dear. Oh dear. Archie is wriggling with embarrassment.

Embarrassment is a kind of fear. Not the kind

you feel when you're stung by a bee or punched by a bully. That fear is physical — it hurts! Not the fear I feel right now at being kicked out of my apartment by Mrs. Ravioli. That's physical too — I'll be living on the street, cold and hungry. Embarrassment is *emotional* fear, which is just as powerful as physical fear. Maybe more. Stress relates to every one of the major causes of death. Right now, Archie is embarrassed because he looks like an idiot. And he panics.

And . . . and . . . it happens.

He sits straight. Swallows. His hair is suddenly neater. His eyes are bigger, brighter, more welcoming. He clears his throat and smiles up at the two thugs in the back of the van.

"Well, uh, *hello*," he says in a voice that is suddenly as smooth and rich as a nine-dollar milkshake.

CHAPTER 20

SORRY, LAURIE

In a matter of seconds, Archie's free. All he had to do was ask.

The van is careening down Davie Street. "Gosh," he says, "I hate to *bother* you. I know you're busy kidnapping us. Kidnapping is a tough job and you guys are good at it. Bravo! Really — give yourselves a pat on the back! It's just that I, well, I *have* to get home. Do you mind? If it's not too much trouble, could you find a place to — well — let me *out*? And could it be, uhhh, *soonish*?"

The driver is happy to oblige. He stops at the corner of Davie and Granville, in the right turn lane with the hazard lights flashing. Archie gets out and speaks through the open side door.

He starts back along Davie. He's got a longer walk home than normal. Bummer. Son of a bletch. Does he think about his missing friend? No.

Archie doesn't remember Uday at all. He is still coming out from under the spell of his superpower. He doesn't know what's going on, just that some time is missing. This doesn't worry him. It's happened before. He's used to forgetting things. He does notice a brand-new sign on the side of a Davie bus: *BC PLACE TOMORROW — UNION DUKE!*

Right, he thinks. *I remember that. I'm going to that.*

The sun is shining in Archie's eyes, and he turns down a side street and gets distracted by the way his hands make spiky shadows on the pavement. Looks like an asterisk when he holds his hands sideways.

It takes him almost an hour to walk home because he stops to buy some potato chips and sits down on a raised tree box to eat them. A shabbily dressed woman comes up to him. Come to think of it, her clothes aren't much shabbier than his, but they are dirtier. And she needs a shower more than Archie does.

"Hi," she says. "Got any change?"

He pats his pocket. Nods. "Yup."

She stands next to him with her cracked and grimy hand out for a moment. "Well, aren't you going to *give* me your change?"

"No," he says. "Why?"

She looks at him. He looks back. "I'm Laurie," she says. "I skipped rope at Edgewood Elementary. What can you do?" Her hand is still out.

"I can spread my fingers out so the shadow looks like an asterisk," he says. "Watch the ground there — see?"

Laurie shakes her head and walks away.

"Arch?" A familiar voice from a few doors down. He turns. Dale comes out of a yoga studio with her mat slung over her shoulder. "What are you doing here?"

He answers truthfully. "I don't know. I found myself way over by Granville and decided to walk back."

Dale is used to Archie not knowing how he has got to places. They head home together, naturally falling into step beside each other.

Laurie from Edgewood is leaning against a building, drinking from a bottle of *Goodlitewow!* As they pass she holds the bottle at arms-length and pours it onto the pavement.

Most of the passing buses advertise the Union Duke concert tomorrow. The Bounderbury marketing team have been busy.

"Are you looking forward to it, Arch?"

"Eh?"

"The concert. It'll make money for the homeless. And Union Duke are cool. You think we'll get to meet them? I like that tall guy who plays bass drum and bass guitar together. What's his name?"

They're at Broughton Street. Archie is about to step off the sidewalk. She pulls him back sharply. "The light is red."

"But I want to cross."

"But it's illegal."

He looks up at her with a smile. "What does that Buddha guy say? The foot feels the foot when it feels the ground. I'm going to feel the foot now." He steps onto the road.

"Arch — you remembered!" Even though the light is still red, there's no one coming, and she hurries after him. *I'll break the rules this once*, she thinks.

"I forget most of the stuff you like to spout, but that one stuck with me. So random. You know? The foot feels the foot — ho ho ho. Buddha was a crazy dude."

The next bus has a poster of the band eating Chompo bars.

"Do you agree with Uday, Arch? Does a viral video prove that you have some kind of gift or superpower?"

"I don't have a superpower. I don't even have a gift. And Doc Fassbinder doesn't think so either."

"Yeah — but stuff has been happening since you got back from Montreal. Uday is sure there's something."

"I don't know if he still thinks so. I didn't sell any pencils. And he's kind of weird anyway."

He wrinkles his brow. Something about Uday. Nope. The memory is gone. Oh well.

"Hey! Uday's our friend, Arch." She strides down the Davie hill toward Denman and English Bay. Eyes squinted against the sun. Jaw set.

"Can't he be both?" Archie calls, struggling after her on shorter legs. "Weird *and* a friend?"

She opens her mouth and closes it. Friendship has rules, like traffic safety. You're not supposed to cross against the light. Or say anything against your friend.

Archie catches up. He's playing with his hands again, pretending he is a giant squid and his fingers are tentacles. "Ho ho!" he says, grabbing hold of Dale's shoulders from behind.

MORAL REASONING

And what *about* Uday? Where is he now? Archie has forgotten him, but he's still part of the story. What's happening? I can answer that.

It's a couple of hours after the kidnap, and Uday is sitting on a couch in the basement of the white clapboard house at the end of 66th Street. He's not tied up or anything. But he can't run away because the two thugs from the van are sitting beside him, holding on to his arms. The van driver is in an armchair.

They are all watching Clemmie Clutterbucket. It's her house, you remember. She's crutching up and down. She's upset. "Where's Archie O'Kaye?" she yells. "*He's* the special kid, Fassbinder's kid. The one from Dimly. The one we want. I gave you a photo to make sure you got the right kid. You had him in the van. But you didn't bring him back. Why?"

The thugs smile, thinking back to their encounter with Archie.

"He told me to stop, so I did," says the driver.

"He told me to open the door," says the woman who watches *Squid Central.* "And I did it. I wanted to do what he said."

"It was the way he asked," says the other thug. "His voice. He was, well, irresistible."

"You brought another kid instead!" yells Clemmie. "What should we do with *him*?"

"*Should*?" says the driver. "Did you ask what we *should* do?"

Wait — let me straighten these guys out for you. Their bank-robber stocking masks are off now and

I can see them better. These two thugs and the driver are Clementine's troops. Her sidekicks. Her henchmen, except that one of them is a woman. Her henchpeople. Which makes Clemmie herself one of The Boss's henchpeople.

The two thugs are named Dex for Dextra and Dix for Dickson. Dextra is the woman who liked Archie's boxer shorts. She's got a round face, dark hair and pale skin. Dix is thinner and even paler. His nose is flatter, like someone punched it a few times.

They call the driver Doc because he really is a doctor — of moral philosophy. He's older than the other two, with shaggy grey hair and darker skin. He looks like a professor, which he was. He lost his job when his university became a technical college. They wanted Doc to switch from teaching moral reasoning to teaching funeral directing, but he couldn't do it. So he quit the university and took the job as Clemmie's driver. He can't forget his training, though. Moral philosophers are always thinking about the right thing to do. They use the word *should* a lot.

"What we *should* do," says Doc, "is make use of *this* boy here. He's Archie's friend. We should find out what he knows about him. That's what we should do."

Uday's listening hard, wondering how to use the situation. Can he make a deal here? Remember, people are more than just one thing. A bully on the playground can be a victim at home. Archie is a scaredy cat — and irresistible — and a bit of a baby. Dale is a dreamer and a do-gooder. Uday is a friend — and he likes Dale — and he's a schemer. Listen to him now. Scheming away.

"Why are you guys all so interested in Archie?" he says. "It's his superpower, right?"

Clemmie corkscrews herself around in an ecstasy of interest. "So there *is* a superpower," she whispers. "I thought so, when I saw the video clip. Tell me more, boy. If he can sell chocolate bars, he can sell drinks."

"I filmed that clip. I'm Archie's best friend."

Clemmie's brain whirls like a figure skater. "The Boss will want to talk to you," she says. "If you can lead us to Archie . . ."

Uday gives a slow smile. This is working out perfectly. "I'll talk to your boss," he says. "But if I lead you to Archie, what do I get out of it?"

So don't worry about Uday. He's fine — for now, anyway. Let's get back to Archie.

☆ ☆ ☆

He's home now, in his mom's living room, playing *Gang of Greats* with Dale. They take turns playing his character in the Forest of Confusion. When it's Dale's turn, Archie goes to the bathroom. When he gets back, Dale is clicking the controller madly.

"How do you get rid of a plague of Gorgs?" she asks.

This is a good life question. Gorgs are all around us.

"Try hiding."

His phone buzzes. A message from Uday: "Don't worry about me." Archie doesn't remember anything about the two of them being kidnapped. He texts back: "OK."

Dale's voice: "It's dark in here. I don't know where the Gorgs are."

"Try a visibility spell."

Frantic clicking.

There's another text from Uday: "I'm free! Don't call cops. Or parents." Archie has no idea what he's talking about. But he doesn't care. Uday will explain sometime. He texts back: "OK."

The clicking stops. "Oh dear," says Dale.

"I've died again, haven't I?"

"Sorry."

Archie shrugs. He likes *Gang of Greats* but he's not very good at it. Gaming is fun the way going on rides is fun. It's not about winning. He likes the weapons and bad guys.

Another message from Uday: "Meet me tomorrow. 8:30 a.m. My place. Side door. I have a plan." More pencils? Archie hopes not. He puts the phone away.

Maeve comes in the front door with dinner from the Thai restaurant around the corner. She turns on the radio and starts getting the meal ready.

"Do you want to stay for dinner, Dale?"

"No thanks, Maeve. I should be going home. See you tomorrow. Maybe in the morning, or at the concert for sure. That'll be fun!"

"Concert?" Maeve smiles uncertainly. "What concert?"

"The charity concert," says Dale. "BC Place, tomorrow night."

"That? I saw it advertised all day long. I didn't know it was—"

"That's *our* concert! Archie's and Uday's and mine. Everyone in my family is going — even my dorky brother, Gradey. Didn't you tell your mom, Archie? Archie!"

He's in the Forest of Confusion, dodging rogue Gorgs. He doesn't answer.

The radio is tuned to CBC. It'd be appropriate if a song by Union Duke was playing right now. But it's news time. They're talking about tax hikes.

CHAPTER 22

WHY DID YOU ABANDON ME?

Now we move to Clemmie's house on 66th Street. She's in the basement writing out a script for tomorrow. The headline says it all: *Why I Love Goodlitewow!*

She hunches and writhes her body over the computer desk for an hour. Then she calls Doc down to help. The former professor is a better editor than Dex and Dax, who are better at kidnapping and torturing. Might as well use your henchpeople to your advantage.

While Doc is typing, Clementine goes to the basement window. The nearly full moon shines down on the backyard. The giant white pole — taller than a football goalpost — gleams silver. The Boss ties up here when she visits. Which won't happen any time soon. Her grey glabrous, saggy, patched, flabby hot-air balloon is steaming toward Toronto right now.

It's late. Really late. So late it's early. The Boss is in her aerial bedroom. But she can't sleep. She's pacing. She's upset. Of course, you can't see The Boss. You can see her nightie, which is cream-coloured with tiny flowers on it and ruffles around the neck. She stops pacing. The nightie is pointing at the inside wall of her bedroom — the direction The Boss is facing. She's staring at the picture on her wall, the framed photo of the round-headed guy with a big swash-buckling moustache. Dr. Fassbinder. She mutters something inaudible to everyone but me, because — well, because I'm the narrator.

"Oh, Edgar," she mutters. Teeny water marks appear just below the neckline of the nightie. Salt water. You can't see The Boss, or her tears, but you can see where they soak into the flannel. "Why did you abandon me?" she whispers. "Oh, Edgar, if only we could be together. If only you loved me the way I still love you! Then I wouldn't have to destroy your work!" A few more water marks appear. The nightie shimmies up and down as The Boss's shoulders shake. A Kleenex moves from the pocket of her nightie to the blank area above the neckline. There's a quiet, delicate honking sound as The Boss blows her nose.

This is what I mean about people being more than one thing. The Boss — a.k.a. Debbie Nussbaum — is an archvillain circling the globe with evil intent. But she is also a sad, lonely woman, neglected by the man she loves. I could almost feel sorry for her. Almost. Hard to feel sorry for someone who wants to destroy four children. I don't feel sorry for the witch in "Hansel and Gretel" either. Or the giant in "Jack and the Beanstalk."

After kissing Dr. Fassbinder's picture, she goes over to her computer and starts typing a script of her own. Nothing to do with the *Goodlitewow!* campaign.

Meanwhile, 3,000 kilometres west and 200 metres down, Uday is sound asleep. He snores slightly and dreams of money, as he often does. Tonight's dream has him in a bathtub, wearing winter clothes. When he turns on the tap, coins come out. And keep coming. The flood of coins covers Uday's boots, outstretched legs and the bottom of his parka, then rises to fill his pockets, then goes even higher to spill over the edge of the tub onto the bathroom floor. Uday does not turn off the tap. The bath mat is covered. The floor is disappearing. Uday smiles.

I think that's all the important people. When everyone wakes up, the sun is shining.

CHAPTER 23

DAISY AND ARCHIE?

"Breakfast!" calls Maeve. She's wearing a bright green top and black pants, with a strand of pearls around her neck. She's more dressed up than usual because she has to make a presentation to the board of Science World this afternoon.

Archie wears the same jeans as yesterday and is about to put on a fresh shirt. It's red, if you care — he doesn't, particularly. It's the one on top of the pile of clean clothes.

Breakfast is toast and grape juice. The sun sketches golden diamonds across the kitchen floor.

"Comb your hair and brush your teeth," says his mom, as she does most days.

He grunts his usual reply.

There's a knock at the door. It's eight fifteen. Dale, not surprisingly, is on time. "I have to ask you something, Maeve," she whispers.

"What is it, Dale?" It's just the two of them in the hall. Archie is at the bathroom sink, holding a toothbrush.

"Do *you* think Archie has a superpower? Uday thinks so, and there are all those hits on the video clip. And some weird things have happened around the school this past week. But I've never seen the video. To me Archie is just his regular self. You live with him and you're his mom. Have you noticed anything?"

Dale checks down the hall. The bathroom door is partly open. Archie is peering into the mirror, making faces at himself.

"I wonder if Dr. Fassbinder made a mistake," she whispers back. "Arch is supposed to be developing some kind of gift, but I haven't seen it yet. I remember barbecues back in Dimly, with the Lundborgs, the Flems and the Kildares, back when the kids were young. I remember one of them falling over, and Gary sneezing and sneezing. No, wait — it was Jess. Cute little thing, but she was like a machine gun. Maybe it was Gary who fell over. Anyway, I never saw any of them do anything super. I'm not in touch with them anymore. Of course, I see Ms. Kildare occasionally, and Daisy goes to your school now. But—"

"Daisy Kildare?" says Dale, in a normal voice. "Daisy is like Archie? She has a gift? She goes to Montreal too?"

"Oops!" Maeve blushes. "Oh dear, that's supposed to be a secret."

"Daisy Kildare?" Dale shakes her head. "I know the art teacher really likes her. In fact, Mrs. Winklehorn was so enthusiastic about Daisy I almost chose Art for my long-weekend activity camp — just to be with her. I don't know about Archie's gift though. Are you sure that's what the testing in Montreal is about?"

"That's what the doctor told me," says Maeve. "I don't know. I've never seen Arch show any special talent. He wanted to go to Nap Camp this weekend. It was a joke, right?"

Dale smiles. "I don't know what his destiny is, but he's developing something special. He got Big Mean Ehsin to give him candy this week. No one has done that before. Everyone in the city — except me — has seen the Chompo video clip. I can't download it."

"Me neither. I've heard a lot about it though."

Funny, isn't it? Dale and Maeve may be the only two people in Archie's life who have never seen him in his superhero mode. They may also be the only ones who like him for who he is. He comes out of the bathroom with his shirt hanging out and his hair all over the place.

"I used that extra-whitening toothpaste," he says. "Can you tell? Does my smile glint?"

Maeve wipes a small glop of toothpaste from his cheek. They say goodbye in the doorway. Maeve will go straight to the concert after her meeting. She and Archie will meet there.

"Don't forget to invite your dad to the concert. Will you do that?"

"Uhhh, maybe. Bye! Got to go." He drags Dale down the hall.

"Say hi to Uday," Maeve calls after them. "And congratulations to the three of you. I'm proud of you, Arch."

Dale smiles back at her. Archie waves without turning around.

CHAPTER 24

USEFUL SHORTCUTS

What's going on with Uday? What is his mystery text all about? You've probably worked it out. Let's follow Archie and Dale and see.

Uday's apartment building is not far away from Archie's. They turn into the laneway between Davie and Drake. Hundreds of laneways criss cross downtown Vancouver. Running behind old factories and apartments, the laneway map is a parallel street map. Laneways make useful shortcuts.

"Why does he want to meet us at the back door?" asks Dale. "What's wrong with the front door?"

Archie never thinks about this kind of question. "That's what he said. Back door."

Dale makes a phone call. "Your dad isn't picking

up," she says. "I know you'll forget to invite him to the concert, so I thought I would. I'll leave a message. Do you think that's bossy of me?"

"Yup."

"Oh dear. I don't want to be bossy."

Archie laughs. "And I don't want to sit behind Willie in math class. Her perfume stinks. She smells like flowers. Anyway, it's too late for both of us. Ho ho ho." You remember that Archie laughs like a teenaged Santa.

As they near Uday's place, Archie's phone buzzes with an alert about a funny video. He checks it out. Dale decides that she wasn't being bossy. Being bossy is wrong, and calling Mr. O'Kaye was the right thing to do, so it can't be bossy.

Archie and Dale walk down the lane behind Uday's building. When they get close they have to stop because a recycling truck is blocking the whole lane. There's only a few centimetres on either side. The children can't get past it. The back end of the truck is open.

"Ew," says Dale.

"Huh?" Archie doesn't look up from his phone. "Did you see this dog with its head in a bucket? See? It looks pretty silly, walking into things. Ho ho ho!"

A white cargo van with *Goodlitewow!* on the door

pulls out of the underground parking lot behind Archie and Dale and stops. Now the lane is blocked ahead of and behind them. Three people get out of the van and run toward them. They grab both phones.

"Hey, I was watching that," says Archie.

Two men and a woman, all wearing noise-cancelling headphones, bundle the children into the truck. Not the cab. The back part. This is a recycling truck, so it's not full of goop, but it's still pretty yucky. The woman pulls on a handle, and the hopper door slides closed.

Dale knows how garbage trucks work. The stuff in the back gets crushed and compacted. "Wait!" she shouts, struggling to escape. "Help!"

The three headphone wearers don't change expression as they push her back into the truck. They can't hear her. The door keeps closing.

"What's going on?" says Archie. "What's that smell?"

The motor stops when the door is almost closed. Dale breathes a sigh of relief. They won't get compacted. There's a thin ribbon of light — a few centimetres — which means that they can breathe. And see a bit.

"I'm sitting on potato chip bags," says Archie. "That's the smell. Barbecue."

(FYI: You know that potato chip wrappers aren't recyclable, don't you? Whoever threw them out made a mistake. It's not important to the story, but I want to be a good citizen. A full-service narrator.)

Dale puts her face up to the gap in the rear door. She can see down the laneway. A familiar figure edges around the front of cargo van and into view. It's Uday! She is about to call out to a warning to her friend, when she notices his pleased smile. She's seen that smile before. Uday slaps one of the headphone guys on the back. The two of them shake hands.

She can't stop herself from yelling. "Uday! You—"

The garbage truck moves forward with a jerk, cutting her off and throwing her back into darkness and the smell of barbecue.

CHAPTER 25

GWWHHUUAAHH!

Let's follow. Not from inside, because it's kind of stinky and dark. We'll hover over top, like we're in a helicopter.

The truck grumbles and rumbles a long way down Granville, turns onto Marine Drive, makes a few more turns, and ends up on 66th Street. The trip takes a long time. Recycling trucks aren't as fast as cars or vans, and the driver — Doc — is not used to the vehicle. I'm afraid it's pretty bumpy and bouncy inside the back. Good thing we're not there.

The truck parks in Clemmie Clutterbucket's drive-way, behind the white *Goodlitewow!* van. The front door of the house opens. Out come Dex and Dix, who were in the van and arrived earlier. With them is another henchperson of Clemmie's, a big round guy with a big round face on top of his big round body. Like a snowman, or that Michelin Tire guy. He's not soft fat. He's strong. His nickname is Dax and that's what they call him. (I've forgotten his real name.) All of them wear those noise-cancelling headphones.

Dax pulls the lever on the side of the recycling truck that opens the hopper at the back. Dale and Archie are dragged into the house and put in handcuffs. Doc moves the truck a few streets over to a big industrial parking lot where someone will find it and report it to the recycling company tomorrow. We're done with it in this story. Back at Clemmie's house, Dale is white faced and silent. Archie is green faced and noisy.

"Worst. Drive. Ever," he says. "I don't want to eat another barbecue potato chip in my whole— Hey. Hey! What are you guys doing? Hey, stop!!"

Dax wraps his arms around Archie from behind, pinning his arms. Dex rips a piece of duct tape with her teeth and covers Archie's mouth. He can breathe through his nose but he cannot speak. At least not normal English.

"Gwwhhuuaahh," he says, through the tape. I know he's saying, "Get this tape off of me," but no one else does. He says a few more things like that. I won't bother translating.

Dex rips off another piece of tape and sticks it on top of the first one. Then a third. Archie is uncomfortable, unhappy and mad.

"Whhahhhhhhhhhhhhuhhhhawayyyiii!" he says.

(You don't want to know what this means. Archie, Archie! I'm surprised you even know those words.)

Dex and Dix take off their headphones.

"What about her?" Dax asks, pointing at Dale.

"Don't worry about her," says Dix.

"What?"

"It's Archie's voice we have to watch out for," says Dex. "He's the irresistible one. Let her alone."

"What?" asks Dax again. He still has his headphones on.

"Why be violent?" asks Dale. "Maybe we would help

you without being tied up and gagged. And what purpose is the gag anyway? Remember what the Buddha says. Three things cannot long be hidden: the sun, the moon and the truth."

Archie says, "Whhaaaahaahaa." He's still mad, but he can't help laughing. He knows how much Dale likes to quote the Buddha.

The henchpeople drag them downstairs. The basement office is a pretty big room, with a couch, chair and computer, remember? Clementine Clutterbucket herself is sitting at the computer. She gets up when the newcomers arrive. She stares at Archie, her eyes like soup bowls, her jaw working as she tries to swallow.

"You," she says at last, thickly, through the phlegm. "At last! I haven't seen you in years."

Archie says, "Eh?" It comes out pretty much like that, even through the duct tape.

"Do you know why you're here? You may think it's punishment. You may think I hate you for being special. No, Archie O'Kaye. The Boss and I want revenge — but not on you or Daisy or Gary or Jessica. Anger is a flame, and I have warmed myself at it for thirteen years. But I am not angry at you. I am angry at Dr. Fassbinder. He set up the reidium experiments. He is the destroyer."

Dale was scared and confused. Now she's also

fascinated. Archie really is special! This twisted lady knows more about Archie's life than he does.

"I lost sight of you when your family left Dimly, Archie O'Kaye. I did not know where you were, or what your power was. Now I do. In Greek mythology, the sirens were dangerous creatures who lured sailors to destruction with the power of their voices. That is your power, Archie O'Kaye. Reidium affected your vocal cords and made you irresistible. You are a siren."

So, the Chompo video was effective because of Archie's mutant vocal cords? Wow. Awesome. But weird. Dale is so interested that she is less scared. Funny how that works — have you noticed?

Archie is lost. He thinks a siren is something on top of a fire truck. He has no idea what Clemmie is talking about. "Whohahwhooay?" he asks, meaning, "What did you say?" He doesn't sound anything like a bewitching sea creature. Greek sailors would be in no danger at all.

"Your mouth is covered so you cannot use your power now. But we will take off the tape. You will work with us," says Clemmie. "You will make a video clip advertising our product. Sales have been terrible, but with your help they will skyrocket and we will prosper. Isn't that delicious irony? The Boss and I get richer and richer because of your power. Dr. Fassbinder will be helping us. Oh my. Oh my."

She starts to laugh. It's quite a performance. Her shoulders shake, her eyes close, her hands clench, her long, rope-thin upper body whips and snarls itself into a knot. Her voice runs up and down the register.

If Archie is the siren from Greek mythology, Clementine Clutterbucket's laugh is more like the one on top of the fire truck.

CHAPTER 26

AND THEN HE GOT MAD

This should be the climax of the story, right? Two of our main characters betrayed by the third and trapped in a basement. Archie forced to use his superpower against his will. Looks like the bad guys are going to get money and revenge. Big scene. High stakes.

So, what happens? Do our heroes defy the villains? Do they escape or fight back?

Nope. They do what they are told. Dale stays quiet and Archie reads the script. And nothing happens.

Uday knows how charming, how fascinating, how downright irresistible Archie can be. Just yesterday he convinced Doc and Dex and Dix to let him go, even though they were supposed to be kidnapping him.

Archie is not irresistible now. Uday can tell. He's

not wearing headphones. He's filming, and he's bored. Archie is as dull as fractions. As dull as a trip to the museum to look at pots.

Time passes.

And more time.

And more.

It's getting on toward afternoon now. Time is evaporating like water on hot pavement. There's a camera set up in the basement of the house on 66th Street. And a microphone. The script is on a lectern in front of the camera.

A newly opened bottle of *Goodlitewow!* sits on a nearby table.

"Ready for take fourteen, Archie?" says Uday, wearily. "Read the script, and then you can go home. Take fourteen."

Archie clears his throat and peers at the lectern. "*Goodlitewow!* is an amazing drink," he says. "It tastes like a better world— You know, I don't even know what that means."

"Come on — read the script, Archie."

"It tastes like a better world— Except it really tastes like poop. I had a sip. This is take fourteen, so I've had thirteen sips already. Plus one at the cafeteria — that's fourteen sips. I know the drink, and poop is what it tastes like. How long do I have to keep doing this, Uday, you weasel?"

You're probably confused. Let me explain. Archie's superpower kicks in when he's scared. It's not working now because he's not scared. *So why isn't he scared?* He should be. He should be panicking. He's been kidnapped. This is pee-your-pants frightening. I'm scared, and I'm only telling the story.

But Archie isn't scared at all, and here's why. He's not scared because he's mad. Archie is mad at the friend who tricked him and betrayed him and sold him to the bad guys. He's mad enough to explode. And you can't be mad and scared at the same time. (Try it — you really can't.) Friend? Not anymore. Uday is an ex-friend.

"Read the script, Archie," he says.

"It tastes like a better world. One gulp and your life

will change. I know. Mine did . . . Uday, you are killing me. You are like a bletch. I bletch all over you. Call this a script?"

The camera is recording everything Archie says. Uday knows he can edit out the things that are not in the script. "Bletch" is not in the script. It's the made-up word those little kids were using yesterday. Uday can take out Archie's mistakes. What he can't do is put in the magic. Archie's superpower is not there.

Archie takes a tiny sip of *Goodlitewow!* — his fourteenth today — shudders, and puts the bottle down hurriedly. (This is the new flavour, tuna fish–espresso. Fresh from the lab.)

Uday stops the camera. The others in the room look a question at him. They're all wearing headphones to keep them safe from Archie's voice. Clementine is wrapped around the computer chair, Dix, Dax and Dex stand on this side of the door, Doc is outside.

They all want to know the same thing. Uday shakes his head. The take didn't work.

This is not a good moment to be Uday. Last night was different. After his video call with The Boss, Uday was the happiest he'd ever been in his life. He was on a winning team. Invisibility — now there was a superpower! He promised to deliver Archie to market *Goodlitewow!* After that, there was something called

Splotnik they were interested in. Uday might even get to meet The Boss on board her blimp.

SCARY MUSIC

And now everything is falling apart. What's wrong with Archie?

Uday holds up a sign for the others: *BREAK 15 MINS.*

Dex tapes Archie's mouth. Everyone takes off their headphones.

"I don't know what to believe." Clemmie stretches her arms out and twists like a tetherball round a pole. "Does he have any power, Uday? Maybe not. Maybe that Chompo thing was a fluke."

Uday shakes his head. "The power is real. But it seems to come and go."

"Let's try The Boss's script," says Clemmie.

CHAPTER 27

MEANWHILE . . .

At Science World, Maeve is teaching a class of students from the international high school about vertebrates. She's having fun. Does she know that her son is tied up and locked in a basement way down at the south end of the city? No. Her heart is light.

From the front of the room she overhears a reference to Union Duke.

"Are you guys fans of the band?" she calls out. "Are you going to the concert tonight?"

Lots of nods and, "Well, yeah!"

"*Si!*"

"*Igen!*"

"Maybe I'll see you," she says. "My son's meeting me there."

"Your son?"

"*Tu hijo?*"

"*A te fiad?*"

Maeve smiles. "Yup. He'll be backstage. With the band."

A jaw drop sounds the same in any language.

An hour later she gets a call from her ex-husband. Would she pass on a message to Archie about the big concert tonight?

"Did Arch phone you? I told him to."

"His friend Dale called. I can't get through to Archie. Would you tell him I have to show a property tonight, so I won't get to the concert."

"Why don't you tell him when you meet him for dinner?" But Ryan has already hung up. Maeve shakes her head angrily.

In fact, Ryan has also forgotten about dinner. Archie is on his own. (Not that dinner is his biggest problem!) Anyway, I think that's the last we'll hear from his dad in this story.

Meanwhile . . . over at Pendrell Public, all the students are still excited from yesterday. The last bell just rang, and kids are working out when they should head over to BC Place to line up for the concert.

CHAPTER 28

ARCHIE O'KAYE IS A HOAX!

Back to the basement of 66th Street. Dax, Dex, Dix and Doc stand in the hall outside the office, keeping watch. Inside, Clemmie sits near the computer, wearing headphones. Dale sits on the floor, wearing handcuffs. Uday runs the camera and mic. Archie holds the second script, the one The Boss worked on late last night. This one is not about *Goodlitewow!*

The computer runs a video call from a faraway blimp.

SCARY MUSIC

That's right. The Boss wants to be there while Archie reads her script. Is he as irresistible as people say? As irresistible as that Chompo video?

"Anytime," says Uday, checking the levels.

Archie begins: "Dr. Edgar Fassbinder — of Pianvia, of Dimly, Manitoba, now of downtown Montreal — is dangerous and must be stopped. His current pet project involves four special children. They were exposed at birth to an isotope of reidium. This isotope has been shown to exhibit psychotropic and physiotropic properties when mixed with gonadotropin-releasing hormone."

Archie makes a real meal of this last sentence. He can't get the words right. And of course he can't understand them. He tries a couple more times, and starts to laugh.

Clemmie watches intently. She knows how important this script is to The Boss. When Archie starts laughing, she shakes her head. She has suspected it for hours but she's sure now. This kid is not a superhero. The Chompo video went viral like the one with the cat dancing, or the fat man on the trampoline. It was a fluke. Uday's scheme will not work. This has been a wasted day. She rips off her headphones and throws them away. "Cut," she says. "Sorry, Boss. Archie O'Kaye is a hoax. Fassbinder's other three may have powers but he does not."

Dale was sitting on the floor. She climbs to her feet with difficulty, since her hands are still cuffed together.

Archie smiles over at her. "Did you hear that stuff? Ganadabooboo? What a riot that was!"

She smiles back. Archie doesn't seem to be a super-hero, despite what that doctor thought. She is relieved. She was right all along.

From the computer comes a terrifying hiss. The Boss is speaking: "Destroy them."

Terrifying to me, anyway. And Dale too. She's scared into silence.

"Eh?" says Archie.

"No one laughs at Nussbaum," hisses the computer.

Did I tell you what she's wearing today? Big red wig, big collar, big red nose, bright-coloured smock. A clown with no face.

Absolutely horrifying.

"NO ONE! Clutterbucket, you have your orders. Do

it now. I will stay online. I want to watch these three children die."

More silence.

"Not me, Boss!" says Uday, rushing over to address the computer screen. "Kill those two, but not me! I'm a traitor, remember? I'm not with them anymore. I'm with you. I got them to come to my back door so you could pick them up. I'm on your side. Let me stay alive. I can help you with *Goodlitewow!* I can help you with Splotnik!"

"Destroy them all," hisses the insane clown Boss, formerly Nurse Debbie Nussbaum, member of a caring profession.

Guess what happens to Archie now? He hears that he is about to die, and—

And—

And—

CHAPTER 29

WHAT'S GOING ON?

Wait a minute! Nothing is happening. Let's try that again. *Ahem.* Archie hears that he is about to die, and— and— and nothing.

What? Nothing? I'm the narrator. It's my story. I know what's supposed to happen. Archie's super-power kicks in, he charms everyone, gets free and saves the day, and the kids make it to the concert. Uday isn't friends with Dale and Archie anymore, and when he gets home all there is to drink is *Goodlite-wow!* That's the way the story goes.

So, why isn't it happening the right way? This is crazy. Against the rules. You don't know what's going to happen next, and neither do I.

NEITHER DO I!

CHAPTER 30

WHAT HAPPENS NEXT?

So, it turns out that I was wrong. That last chapter wasn't the climax. *This* is the climax. I mean, destroy them? It can't get more dire than that. Can it? Let's find out.

Clementine draws herself up as straight and as high as she can. "Dax, Dex, Dix, Doc!" she calls. "Here."

They come rushing into the room.

"What can we do?" ask Dax and Dix and Dex.

"What *should* we do?" asks Doc.

Clemmie points at the children. Dale shrinks away from the pointing finger. She knows. Uday cringes and whimpers. He knows. Archie doesn't do anything. He doesn't know. I guess that's why his superpower isn't working.

He's not scared. He should be, but he's not. He doesn't see that he's in danger. He's still giggling at "ganadabooboo."

"Destroy them!" says Clemmie. "Crush them, slice them, evaporate them. Make them disappear! Use your hands. Use whatever weapons you have, whatever machines you can find. Do it here and now. The Boss wants to watch."

"Yesssssssssssss," from the computer.

Doc hesitates. Should they do this? Should they really? Dex and Dax and Dix are simple and obedient. If The Boss wants them to kill children, they'll do it. They move forward in a circle. Lubomir — I just remembered Dax's real name, and Lubomir sounds more menacing — has his arms outstretched. He's strong enough to crush the life out of anyone.

Wow — I did not see the story ending this way. Are you surprised? Me too!

Dale turns her back on Uday, the traitor. She would be mad at him if she could, but she is too frightened to feel anger as well. (You can't feel them both together, remember?) She reaches out to Archie.

"Look!" he says, pointing. The desk lamp by the computer throws the shadow of Dale's hand up on the wall. "Cool, eh? Your hand shadow looks like a camel," he says. "Doesn't it?"

"Arch—"

"Or is it a weasel? Or maybe a whale? Yeah. The back is like a whale."

He is so oblivious to the threat, so pure in his ignorance, that it's a kind of greatness. Dale is moved. She leans down so that her head is level with Archie's. And kisses him, pretty hard, on the corner of his mouth.

Uday groans. This is what he wanted to happen to him. And now it won't. He chose scheming instead of loyalty, and his choice has come back to hurt him.

Archie is young for his age. He likes Dale as a friend, a pal, a girl down the street. If he's in love with her, he doesn't know it. He thinks girls are icky. When she kisses him, Archie is immediately, completely, monumentally embarrassed. It's as if he has walked out of the house with no clothes on, or farted loudly in the middle of a math test. That's how embarrassed he is.

The kiss is going on and on. Someone else being there, seeing it, makes his embarrassment worse. And who is the someone else? Uday! Another *guy* — a guy he's mad at, a guy he's known a long time. *No wonder he groaned*, thinks Archie. *He sees how stupid I look.*

Embarrassment, as you know, is a kind of fear. Archie did not even notice the threat from the forces who wanted to destroy him. But he is so embarrassed by Dale's kiss that he panics. Panic hormones pour through his body, from hair to toes and everywhere in between.

And—

And—

And—

Oh my gosh! Now it happens.

"Well, *hello* there!" he says, smiling around the room. Remember how white his teeth were this morning after brushing? They're even whiter now. "I don't know if I, er, *remember* all your names. I should. My fault, definitely. But, er, there it is. I'm Archie, of course. Hi." He sketches a diffident wave.

"Now, most of you are old friends, but *you—*" turning to Clementine now "—are someone I'd like to get to know better. What an *arresting* presence. The way you make your eyes burn like live coals — that is quite a feat. Do you, er, *practise* that or does it come to you naturally? Really, I can — gosh, I can hardly tear myself away from you. And I don't even know your name! Think of that!"

Picture your first crisp, chewy bite of a hard frozen Popsicle. Got it? Now picture that same Popsicle fifteen minutes later on a hot, hot, hot day, as you lean toward it, and it's drooping and dripping, sweet and soft and sticky. Clementine's heart is that Popsicle. Archie's personality is the sun. She melts.

"My name," she says, in a trembling voice, "is Clementine."

"I know that name! In a cavern," he sings, right away, right on pitch, "in a canyon, excavating for a mine. Lived a miner, forty-niner, and his daughter Clementine." His laugh is smallpox. It is the bubonic plague. They all catch it.

Archie's charm comes in reaction to a threat, remember. He uses charm like a weapon. The Boss is the biggest threat. She's on the other end of the video conference. But he can't see her. All he can think to do is smile at the screen.

"You should go away now," he says, softly, intimately, speaking soul to soul. "If you do, you'll be happier. Edgar will be happier too. After all, he's the one you—"

The screen goes blank. The Boss has shut down the video call. Will we see her again in this story? I don't think so. I really don't. Mind you, I'm not as all-knowing a narrator as I thought.

How does Archie remember Fassbinder's first name? How does his hair comb itself? How does his shirt tuck itself in? Seems like magic. That's how superpowers work, right? Physiotropic (is that even a word?), like The Boss says.

Speaking of threats, selling *Goodlitewow!* was a problem a while ago. It isn't a problem now, but Archie solves it anyway. He can't help himself, any more than the Hulk can. *Hulk smash! Archie charm.*

There's still an open bottle of *Goodlitewow!* on the table by the video camera. The camera that is running. Archie picks up the bottle. Smells it as if he appreciates it. Smiles at the camera.

"Mmmm," he says. "Strawberry. And tuna. And espresso. Together at last. This. Is. Amazing. You know what you should do? All of you out there? You should drink some."

He holds it up to the camera, but before he can take a sip, he stumbles and drops the bottle. It breaks. Looking down at the broken bottle, Archie cries. Can you imagine how effective this video clip might be?

Dix is licking his lips. "Do you know where there's more of that stuff?" he whispers, gesturing to the broken bottle. "I want some."

"Me too," says Dex.

"Let's go to my place!" yells Uday suddenly. "I want some too and my nani bought a whole case!"

"You know what we *should* do?" says Doc, leading the rest of them up the stairs. "We should all get in the *Goodlitewow!* van and drive to Uday's!"

So they do. Clementine, Lubomir (sorry, Dax), Dex, Dix, Uday, Dale and Archie make seven passengers. The trip uptown is quicker than the one down. Sun on their left, dodging behind the big buildings as they get closer to downtown. Archie keeps up a steady stream of charm. It cascades out of him — words, gestures, attitudes — like water from a firehose. Doc dodges through the traffic. He's in a hurry.

Dale has been pretty quiet ever since she kissed Archie. She stares at him now and then, the way you stare at a butterfly that was a chrysalis only minutes ago. "What happened?" she whispers. "Who are you now? It's like you've woken the Buddha within you."

He takes her hand and gives it a squeeze. He's never done that before.

Where Cambie Street hits Pacific, you can see BC

Place on the right. Traffic slows to a crawl, and then a stop. Bounderbury trucks are parked on the sidewalk at the south side of the stadium, and a crowd of mostly kids mills about, getting free chocolate. Tonight's show begins soon.

Doc wants to turn left to get to the west end and Uday's. But they're stuck. No one moves.

Dale puts her hand on the door handle. A turn, a pull, and the door slides open.

"Gosh, what a good idea! I was about to suggest getting out right here," says Archie, with a dazzling smile. "We really should go to that concert."

No cars are moving. The two of them exit the van together. From the road, Archie turns back to talk to the passengers.

"Keep hold of *this* guy," he says to Dex, Dax and Dix, pointing at Uday. "He's got some *Goodlitewow!* for you at his place. Clementine, you are not lost and gone forever. There's a million sales in the camera at your place. I expect to see the clip online in a day or two. When The Boss calls, say hi for me. Now, Doc, let me clear the traffic for you here. Hey! Hey!"

Archie knocks on the windows of cars in the next lane. Gestures widely. "Move over! All of you! You have room. Let this van through. Make a lane, make a lane. Okay, Doc, you should go now. On down the road!"

As the sliding door closes and the van pulls ahead into clear space, you can hear them all saying, "What a guy! What a guy!"

Archie and Dale cross toward the stadium hand in hand.

CHAPTER 31

ANYTHING ELSE?

The story has to end soon. There are only a few pages left. We're at the concert, where I thought we'd be, but I didn't think we'd get here this way. Will I be surprised again? Maybe. Let's move forward. We'll be surprised together.

BC Place is jammed full. Union Duke would probably sell it out anyway, and the extra few thousand seats courtesy of the Bounderbury website make for a sure thing. The band pre-sells three thousand copies of the album they are still recording. The tentative title: *CHOMPO!*

The guru from chapter one — the guy who's been on Oprah — starts everything off with a prayer for the end of anger: "In the words of our Lord Buddha,

You will not be punished for your anger, you will be punished by your anger."

Dale stands in the wings with a few dozen other special guests, watching the stage, thinking angry thoughts about Uday. When she hears Buddha's words she gulps. The guru stays onstage for the first song, surprising everyone by clapping in time and mouthing the words. He's clearly a fan.

By the third song, Archie has come back from wherever he was. He is no longer his irresistible self. He's just Archie.

Of the last hour he remembers nothing. "We were in that basement, and Uday was filming me. There was a bunch of funny long words that didn't mean anything. And then you leaned over. That's the last thing I remember."

"Really?" says Dale, flushing a little.

"Uh-huh."

From the wings, they are close enough to see the tall, calm bass player's freckles, and the manic lead singer's small tattoo.

"I don't understand," Dale says in Archie's ear. "You made sense. You talked them into driving us away from that horrible house. You saved us all. Even Uday. I heard you. It was amazing."

"Okay, but I don't remember any of it."

"None at all? You really don't remember me — doing *anything* to you?"

"Doing what? Nope. Nothing."

He's forgotten the kiss. She hoped it would mean something to him. But it's gone. "How come? Why don't you remember?"

"I dunno!" He throws his hands up. "Geez, Dale, how can you know what you don't know?" Not much she can say to answer that.

The band sings close harmony on the third verse of a gentle song.

"Well, anyway, I finally saw it. I saw your superpower. Connecting. Making people like you and do what you say."

"*My* superpower? How is it mine? That irresistible guy you're talking about has nothing to do with me."

Onstage, the band hums the chorus. The crowd hums along, enjoying quietly.

Dale shakes her head. "It's you, Archie," she murmurs. "The real you. We all have a superpower inside — a part of ourselves that comes out in crisis. It's not just you and Daisy and the other two. We all have something. It's just that yours is more — well — epic."

"Irresistible? Call that a superpower?"

"You always say what you think, Archie — stuff other people would be afraid to say. It's your truth. It's why I like you. And your superpower is you being more like you. You make the truth compelling."

The song ends. "I dunno," Archie shouts over the applause. "I'd rather fly. Or move things with my mind. That'd be cool. What do they call that?"

"So, if you don't remember being irresistible, you don't remember what got you started — what turned you into the superhero?"

"I don't remember any of it."

"I wonder," says Dale.

"What?"

"If I can ever be friends with Uday again. He totally betrayed us and put us in danger."

Archie shrugs. "I guess I'm still mad at him. But not as mad as I was."

"I wonder about you too, Archie."

"Really? What do you wonder . . . about? You said you . . . like me."

The next song kicks up — a real bouncy one. The banjo goes crazy. Dale and Archie and the other special guests jump up and down together.

It's too loud to talk and Dale doesn't finish telling Archie what she wonders about. But I can tell you. *Did her kiss bring out his superpower?* That's what she's wondering.

We'll leave them for now, more confused than

anything else. This is not a fairy tale, where the prince and princess save the kingdom and get married and live happily ever after. This is a little bit more like normal life. Archie has learned something about who he is, and he's with his best friend, and there will be ice cream in a couple of hours. That's pretty good, right? It's where I thought the story would go.

What's coming up? Let's see. An invitation from Department C (remember them? They funded Dr. Fassbinder's reidium experiments) will arrive in the mail in a week or so.

Archie O'Kaye
YOU'RE INVITED!
If you're reading this you survived ~~your mission~~.
Congratulations!
To celebrate a year of (mostly) successful projects, come to our midsummer potluck picnic for those still alive.
Let us know if you'll bring salad, sandwiches or dessert. (And also cheese.)
Looking forward to seeing whoever is left.

Bernard Cheeper,
Department C Projects Coordination

PS You can bring one guest.

Archie will have no idea what's going on. Why is Department C throwing a picnic? He'll ask Dale what she thinks. Maybe she'll want to come too.

By the day of the picnic, a recent upload from The Boss will reach a million hits. The video is less than a minute long. It's called *Goodlitewow!*

Anything else? Nope? Okay. I guess this is where we say goodbye and . . . No, wait!

Wait!

Why are we heading out over the stage, past the band, into the audience. We're in the second level now. What is going on? Is there one last surprise?

☆ ☆ ☆

"Excuse me. I think this is mine."

"I wondered! It may be the only empty seat in the house."

"Section 214, seat D4. Yup, that's me."

"The show has already started."

"Yeah. I'm running late. I just had to finish this story I'm writing. Union Duke is a great band, eh? And it's such a good cause."

"I know! My son is involved. He's one of those kids off to the side of the stage."

"You must be very proud of him."

"I sure am. But wait — have I met you? I feel I know you, somehow." She turns in her chair and stares right at me.

"You should know me. I'm the narrator."

"What?"

"Maybe author would be easier."

"Arthur?"

Like in the bestseller she was reading? Oh, this is too perfect.

"Sure," I say.

"Well, hi, Arthur, I'm Maeve. Glad you're here."

"Me too, Maeve," I say. "Let's enjoy the show."

Onstage, the band starts a fast song. The lead singer's arm moves so vigorously that his tambourine sounds like a jackhammer. I can see Archie and Dale dancing off to the side. She seems lost in the music. Now that I'm in the story, I don't know what he's thinking about for sure. But it's probably ice cream.

DEPARTMENT C HAS BIG NEWS!

IF YOU'RE BURNING A TIRE FACTORY WE ALREADY KNOW. WHAT STINKS?

THE CHEESE DIP, MAYBE?

CHEESE! YIPPEE!

GOUDA

UH-OH. ARCHIE'S SCARED OF MICE.

POP!

HEY, I KNOW THAT GUY.

IS HE COMING TO THIS FUNERAL TOO?

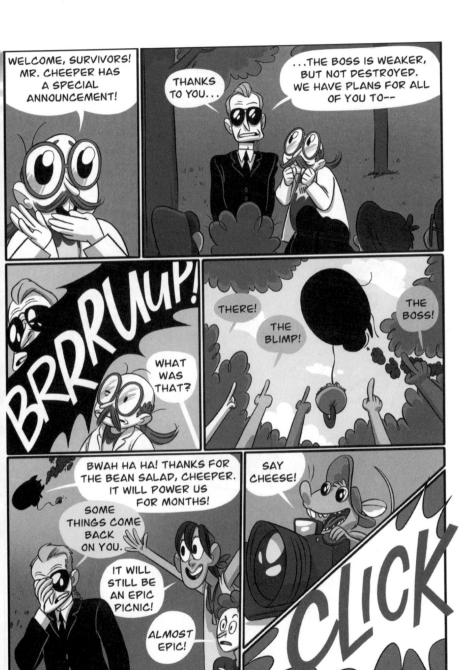

185

Acknowledgements

Talk about a team effort! It's been tons of fun to talk and plan and giggle (it sure doesn't seem like work) with Kevin, Lesley and Ted, from whom ideas flow thick and fast and goofy. Britt's pix capture the flavour of the quartet perfectly. Shout-out to Scholastic sales, marketing, Book Fairs and Clubs, management, design, and editorial (especially Erin for finding the logic in the series). More than anyone else, thank you (thank you, thank you!) to Anne, who's been on board from the start, tucking this baby under her arm and running it back for a touchdown. Yes, I said that.

RICHARD SCRIMGER is the award-winning author of more than twenty books, including *Zomboy, Lucky Jonah* and *Downside Up.* He is also a contributor to the popular Seven series. When he's not writing or talking about writing, Richard teaches at Humber College and gets laughed at by his children. He lives in Toronto. Richard's personal superpower involves line selection. Put him in any supermarket and he will unerringly head for the slowest line, the one that allows you to check email, paint your nails and do your taxes all before it's your turn . . .

FOUR BOOKS.
FOUR AUTHORS.
FOUR UNFORGETTABLE
SUPERHEROES.

Irresistible by Richard Scrimger
Hey, look, you're holding it in your hand!

Mucus Mayhem by Kevin Sylvester
Jessica Flem is allergic to everything except video games.
She's used to a nose that never stops running, but is not
prepared for the mysterious power that shows up around
her thirteenth birthday. Could there be a use for all those
snot-filled tissues? She's about to find out . . .

What Blows Up by Ted Staunton
Gary "Clumsborg" Lundborg is more than a little surprised
to suddenly find himself moving objects with his mind
— not gracefully, often distractedly, and only between
three and six in the morning. Will this help him become a
basketball star? Well, first he must save the world . . .

Super Sketchy by Lesley Livingston
Daisy Kildare is starting over at a new school. Sometimes
she wishes she could be anywhere else. But when she uses
a certain pencil, Daisy finds she can *turn into* whatever
she draws. She just needs to harness that power. If only
her drawing skills were a little more accurate . . .

Visit www.scholastic.ca/almost-epic
for chapter excerpts, videos and more!